GRANTA

12 Addison Avenue, London W11 4QR | email: editorial@granta.com
To subscribe go to granta.com, or call 020 8955 7011 (free phone 0500 004 033)
in the United Kingdom, 845-267-3031 (toll-free 866-438-6150) in the United States

ISSUE 144: SUMMER 2018

PUBLISHER AND EDITOR	Sigrid Rausing
DEPUTY EDITOR	Rosalind Porter
POETRY EDITOR	Rachael Allen
DIGITAL DIRECTOR	Luke Neima
ASSISTANT EDITOR	Francisco Vilhena
SENIOR DESIGNER	Daniela Silva
EDITORIAL ASSISTANTS	Eleanor Chandler, Josie Mitchell
SUBSCRIPTIONS	David Robinson
MARKETING MANAGER	Simon Heafield
PUBLICITY	Pru Rowlandson
TO ADVERTISE CONTACT	Charlotte Burgess, charlotteburgess@granta.com
FINANCE	Mercedes Forest, Josephine Perez
SALES MANAGER	Katie Hayward
IT MANAGER	Mark Williams
PRODUCTION ASSOCIATE	Sarah Wasley
PROOFS	Katherine Fry, Jess Kelly, Lesley Levene, Louise Tucker
CONTRIBUTING EDITORS	Daniel Alarcón, Anne Carson, Mohsin Hamid, Isabel Hilton, Michael Hofmann, A.M. Homes, Janet Malcolm, Adam Nicolson, Edmund White

28 SEPTEMBER – 24 NOVEMBER 2018

DONMAR®

Measure for Measure

BY
WILLIAM SHAKESPEARE

Hayley Atwell and Jack Lowden alternate the roles of the powerful Deputy and powerless Novice within every performance of Shakespeare's exploration of sex and power.

CAST INCLUDES
HAYLEY ATWELL | **JACK LOWDEN**

DIRECTOR **JOSIE ROURKE**
DESIGNER **PETER MCKINTOSH**
LIGHTING DESIGNER **HOWARD HARRISON**

DONMARWAREHOUSE.COM | 020 3282 3808
DONMAR WAREHOUSE, 41 EARLHAM STREET, LONDON WC2H 9LX

Supported using public funding by
ARTS COUNCIL ENGLAND

This production is supported by an anonymous donor

Celebrating **10 YEARS** of partnership

 BARCLAYS

National Art Pass___ _can lead to the unexpected

Georgie King
Individual

Please show your card for free admission and reduced price entry to participating museum and galleries

See more art for less.
Search National Art Pass.

_with Art Fund

Art Fund is the operating name of National Art Collections Fund, a charity registered in England and Wales 209174 and Scotland SWC038331. National Art Pass is issued to Art Fund members. Subscriptions start from £67.

National Centre
for Writing

Sign up for news, events, courses and features at:

nationalcentreforwriting.org.uk

AT THE OLD VIC

2018–2019 SEASON PART ONE

**PRINCIPAL PARTNER
ROYAL BANK OF CANADA**

SYLVIA
**ZOO NATION:
THE KATE PRINCE COMPANY**
03–22 SEPTEMBER 2018

17c
BIG DANCE THEATER
CONCEIVED BY
ANNIE B-PARSON
26–29 SEPTEMBER 2018

WISE CHILDREN
ANGELA CARTER
ADAPTED BY
EMMA RICE
08 OCTOBER–10 NOVEMBER 2018

A CHRISTMAS CAROL
A VERSION BY
JACK THORNE
27 NOVEMBER 2018–19 JANUARY 2019

AND LATES / VOICES OFF / FAMILIES
FOR MORE INFORMATION & TO BOOK PLEASE VISIT OLDVICTHEATRE.COM

PREVIEWS
PARTNER

PRODUCTIONS
PARTNER

IN ASSOCIATION
WITH

PRINCIPAL PARTNER

pwc

THE
PUBLIC FUND

Bloomberg
Philanthropies

RBC

Royal Bank of Canada

CONTENTS

Introduction

This issue of *Granta* is about patriarchy, and some of the ways in which our gendered culture is now creakily changing. We are not attempting to sum up the current feminist movement – all the usual caveats about (mis)representation apply. But the stories in this collection do all address questions of gender.

We begin with Fernanda Eberstadt's memoir, 'I Bite My Friends'. Fernanda was only fourteen when she befriended Stephen Varble, a downtown twenty-eight-year-old drag performance artist. Her liberal Upper East Side parents allowed her to wander into the late 1970s New York scene of drag and chains and leather; that intense countercultural performative space that hardly exists any more, decimated by Aids and tamed by gentrification, antidepressants and marriage equality. What can we say about this young teenager and this hungry activist? Who bit whom? Stephen did once ask Fernanda to suck his dick, but that was probably a joke, and didn't happen. Mostly they seem to have talked, endlessly – they talked each other up, as friends did in those days. All the amazing things they were going to do.

Sally Rooney's two protagonists in the excerpt from her forthcoming novel *Normal People* are friends, too, but the undertone is much darker. Rooney forensically examines the balance of power between her two characters, quietly weighing up all the factors involved.

There is otherwise little friendship between men and women here. TaraShea Nesbit describes her sexual encounters, aged thirteen, with a man old enough to be her father. She vividly captures her persona at the time: a girl not mature enough to understand the manipulative nature of her predator. Stella Duffy interiorised a sense of the helplessness of the man who pawed her as a young girl, and notices that she still wants to protect him: 'Like countless other women, I am willing to out myself, but not the perpetrator. We are trained into silence, trained to protect men from their poor, hapless, helpless selves.'

Their poor, hapless, helpless selves, indeed. But let's not forget how brutal and lonely gender oppression can be. In these pages, Lisa Wells finds a way to remember being sexually abused as a child, and Debra Gwartney describes her botched, and secret, abortion.

Getting treatment for an abscessed tooth was the code, she later came to understand. This was the late 1970s, and still no one in Gwartney's student circles talked about it.

Miriam Toews's next novel is based on the true story of a series of brutal rapes in a Mennonite community in Bolivia. The women are painstakingly trying to process what has happened to them, and decide what they must do. But it's not just heaven and hell that are unknown to them – the real world, even a few miles beyond their farmland, is terra incognita, and the women are more or less trapped in a system of oppressive and archaic patriarchy.

B oth of our photoessays address gender and the question of fluidity: femininity and masculinity in the making. 'Cross-Dressers' is part of a collection of found photographs put together by French film-maker Sébastien Lifshitz; 'Chameleon', by Tomoko Sawada, consists of a series of staged self-portraits. The projects are serious yet curiously light-hearted – humour vs accusations of humourlessness is of course one of the cultural pivots of feminism and gender rebellion. In honour of that at times forgotten binary opposition, here is a joke from Tommi Parrish's graphic story about Figure 1 and Figure 2, and their relationship:

> Figure 1 is an artist of mounting acclaim. At 36 Figure 1 will say to their therapist that they have always used art to dissociate from life. The therapist will nod gently and ask how this makes Figure 1 feel. 'It makes me feel nothing', Figure 1 will say in annoyance. 'That's obviously the whole point.'

There is much to say about the current feminist movement, or moment, but Parrish's 'genericlovestory' captures something interesting about the current zeitgeist – an un-gendered, blandly therapeutic world, yet still so weirdly funny.

We are nowhere near gender parity. But perhaps at least we are travelling in the right direction. ∎

Sigrid Rausing

Fernanda Eberstadt and Stephen Varble shooting *The Immaculate Consternation* at his loft, New York, 1976
© GREG DAY

I BITE MY FRIENDS

Fernanda Eberstadt

This is a story about New York in the 1970s. A broken, genderfuck
friendship story.

When I was fourteen years old and an aspiring writer, my best
friend was a twenty-eight-year-old drag queen and performance
artist named Stephen Varble. I was in the ninth grade at Brearley, an
all-girls school on the Upper East Side, and at that point Stephen was
really the only boy I knew. For almost three years, we explored the
seedier undersides of the city; he introduced me to cocaine and kissing
and to John Waters' star Divine, and I provided him, grudgingly, with
something approaching home. We charmed, wounded, infuriated
each other, squabbled and made up, but even in our most exasperated
moments, we each had this weird faith in our friendship as a kind of
artistic endeavor: I interviewed Stephen about his work, recorded in
my diary every conversation, every meeting; we wrote poems about
each other; Stephen commissioned a photographer friend to make a
film of the two of us, of which only two stills survive. He called me
'Nenna Fiction'.

I went away to college, and stopped answering Stephen's letters.
He became a religious recluse, got Aids, and died; later he was
forgotten because his art was so militantly ephemeral, and because
most of the photographers who documented his performances also

died of Aids and were forgotten. Now both he and they are being rediscovered, and the first museum show devoted to Stephen Varble's work is opening in New York in September this year. It's taken me forty-odd years to be able to begin thinking about this friendship, which is also a story about Aids, genderqueer art, and a city that not so long ago offered possibilities of wild, unsurveilled freedom and experimentation.

It's Easter Sunday, Fifth Avenue. The year is 1975. By the seventies, the Easter Parade's gone from being a society ritual – John D. Rockefeller walking his family to church – to carnival kitsch: couples wearing Easter bonnets the size of grand pianos, Latina triplets in hot-pink lace tap-dancing outside St Patrick's.

My own Easter's been – so far – pretty quiet. I'm cutting across Fifth Avenue at 59th, a pale baby-faced adolescent dressed in a sailor's peacoat and white canvas Keds, on my way home from seeing Buñuel's *The Phantom of Liberty* at the Paris. (The Paris, cater-corner to the Plaza Hotel, had a side entrance you could sneak through if the movie was R-rated.)

I used to go to the movies a lot on my own – to Rogers and Astaire double bills at Theater 80 St Marks, to Truffaut movies at the Carnegie Hall Cinema, and to the Anthology Film Archives to see films by Jack Smith, who'd been a friend of my mother's.

I did a lot of things by myself as a kid. There was some damage in me that meant I found other people's company exhausting. I thought it was my business to be solitary, a watcher, that that was what writers were.

The Easter Parade is winding down, when I spot Him. Her. Them. The Apparition. The Apparition is a bearded young man, lunar-white except for the lavender-and-pink eye makeup. He's wearing a headdress of half-burnt wooden matches crowned by a souvenir matador and bull, a gown made of golden Seagram's V.O. labels, and a pair of black evening pumps. He is on the arm of a mustachioed cowboy in black leather, and he's performing this silent movie pantomime: sidle, shimmy, eyelash flutter, ogle. A small crowd surrounds him.

The thing is, I know him already. I'd clocked the Apparition a month earlier at a Tibetan evening at St Mark's Church-In-The-Bowery, drifting up the aisle in a white wool cassock, with a shredded paperback of the novel *Forever Amber* strapped open across his forehead like an Orthodox Jew's tefillin, its pages fluttering. Odder still, I'm carrying a photo of him in my wallet, clipped from the *SoHo Weekly News*. I don't know his name, but already he's in there with my hottest fetishes, and I know we belong together in some way.

I pass the leather cowboy my newspaper clipping, and now the Apparition's doing her tricks just for me. 'What's your name, little girl?' she whispers in this Southern drawl. She's surprised to see a kid like me at the Easter Parade. 'It used to be real festive, but now it's all RIFF RAFF!' – her voice hiking up to a gargled shriek.

She's right. The mood's turned hostile – a gang of Puerto Rican men has moved in, catcalling, baiting. A soda can is thrown, just misses. The two policemen watching don't do a thing. This random violence from strangers will become familiar to me, tripping along the streets of Lower Manhattan, the Rockaways – worst of all, Staten Island – arm in arm with a bearded man dressed in ballgowns made of garbage: it's part of the perspectival whiplash entailed when a child of privilege falls in with someone from the wrong side of the socio-sexual tracks.

The Apparition, unfazed, bats her eyelashes at this jeering circle of males, except that suddenly she and the cowboy have disappeared down a subway entrance, and me along with them. We're on a downtown train, and the Apparition is taking me home to his.

Stephen Varble had been in New York six years when we met. He was born in 1946 in Owensboro, Kentucky. There are still a lot of Varbles in Owensboro. Judging by YouTube postings, if your name is Varble, you are most likely to seek fame as an evangelical preacher or a bluegrass banjo player. (There is also a fifty-one-minute film on YouTube of Stephen dancing in the disco Hurrah, naked beneath a costume made of bead curtains and a life preserver stolen from the Staten Island Ferry.)

Stephen's family were stalwarts of the Audubon Church of the Nazarene, his father had some kind of real-estate business, and Stephen was a mamma's boy, but he must have known pretty early he had to hightail it to a big city. He graduated Phi Beta Kappa from the University of Kentucky, and arrived in New York 'with seven dollars and a pretty face', he later told me. He waited tables at the ice-cream parlor Serendipity, and supposedly was fired for performing stripteases for the customers, but also got his master's in film from Columbia. Straightaway, he encountered Jack Smith, another bearded costume queen whose baroque bacchanalia shot on damaged film stock went right into Stephen's bloodstream; he performed in Fluxus happenings; his plays were produced at Lincoln Center and La MaMa. These are the building blocks of a mainstream arts career, but already there was something virulently anti-institutional in Stephen's ethic that made him sabotage any glimmer of even supposedly 'indie' success.

By the time we met in the spring of 1975, Stephen was practicing what he described as Gutter Art: street performances in costumes concocted from materials he found in the dumpster. Sometimes these performances involved corralling passersby into guerrilla 'tours' of the SoHo galleries; sometimes he had himself driven around town by his patron Morihito Miyazaki in a Rolls-Royce, wearing an Elizabethan-style hooped skirt constructed from egg cartons, and stopping outside strategic sites – the Metropolitan Museum, say – to wash a stack of dishes in the gutter. In Stephen's most famous action, staged a year after we met, he flounced into a branch of Chemical Bank, wearing a gown made of dollar bills, with breasts formed by twin condoms filled with fake blood. Shrieking that someone had forged a million-dollar check in his name and he wanted the money back 'Now! Now! Now!', Stephen exploded his condom-breasts like a gender jihadi and began writing checks with the blood.

What do you do with an artist whose politics are expressed with such whimsical coquettishness that you could mistake his assault on capitalism and the art industry for mere camp? This was class warfare, though Stephen would say that *his* dispossessed were the natural aristocrats dismayed by the tackiness of contemporary commerce. Like Diogenes, the ancient Greek philosopher who is the godfather of political street art, Stephen had come to debase the currency.

We are sitting on the M train, me, Stephen in his golden Easter Parade dress, and the leather-clad cowboy, headed to Stephen's apartment on the Lower East Side. The cowboy, Stephen's off-and-on lover, is called Robert Savage, and he's shy to the point of mutism. He's an experimental composer who works in a jewelry store 'to satisfy his insatiable *passion* for opals', Stephen explains. 'He's kinda mystical, but we don't have sex anymore because he does *awful* things to himself: he's a self-castrator. He carries on these long, secret blood rituals – draining his veins and sticking things up his urethra to make the blood gush out. He's always getting hospitalized, with blood streaming.' Leaning closer, Stephen confides, '*He can't even beat off anymore!*'

Robert, silent, grinds the heels of his black policeman shoes into the subway-car flooring.

I look at Robert sideways with an unsettled kind of fellow feeling. Sex scares me rigid. Soon as my child's body sprouted unwanted breasts, middle-aged men had started rubbing themselves against me on buses, murmuring obscenities. Home is no refuge: since I was little, my mother's bedtime stories have been about the different things she likes to get up to with her boyfriends.

My reaction to all this sexual terror has been to become obsessed with gay male strangers, whom I stalk at a safe distance. Only by keeping everything in my head, with multiple barriers against consummation, can I feel some control. It will take me some time to realize that I'm not just attracted to gay men, I want to *be* one. I've gone from dreaming myself Tom Sawyer to dreaming myself Tom of Finland.

Today, my adolescent self might be tempted to identify as genderqueer – Stephen, I am guessing, would have found the whole notion of 'identifying' drearily bureaucratic – but back in 1975, this attraction to an outlaw tribe from which I was excluded felt somewhere between tag-along embarrassing and insane.

No more insane, though, than wanting to drain your own blood or dress up in garbage.

Stephen's studio, above a Chinese takeout on Delancey Street, resembles a backstage costume room, with wardrobe racks and a dressmaker's dummy and a giant, pink satin mattress on the floor. Stephen and Robert and I roll all over it and tickle each other with pink feather-puff pillows, till Stephen announces, 'I'm so ravenous I could eat this pillow and lick my fingers afterwards.' He's biting each knuckle hard in quick succession – 'That keeps them kinda staring and agonized-looking' – but his self-cannibalism is also hunger. He's often hungry, and mostly I'm too well fed myself to respond to the hints.

Luckily, tonight my weekly allowance is still intact, so Robert and I watch Stephen change to a pair of Levi's and a plaid flannel shirt – he's constantly code-switching from Marie Debris, his costume-queen alter ego, to butch-er styles of queerness – and I treat him and Robert to dinner at the Star of Bengal, which is Stephen's 'favorite place in the wo-orld because they serve pomegranate cocktails that make you *scream*', he says, letting out a ladylike caterwaul. I am quietly soaring, it's one of those moments when a kid thinks: my real life, the life I've always dreamed of, has just begun.

In the spring of 2016, I came upon a Peter Hujar photograph of Stephen from his Chemical Bank action. Eyes half closed in swooning bliss, luscious lips parted in a roguish smile, he brandishes a check made out to Peter Hujar for 'zero million dollars'.

My heart crashed.

It had been decades since I'd thought of Stephen. The last time we met, after a long break, was in 1982, and ever since, as the Aids epidemic raged and gentrification erased all his old habitats, I'd blanked him from my consciousness. Wondering what had happened to Stephen would have meant admitting that he must have died of Aids – why else wouldn't I have heard from him in all these years?

I googled 'Stephen Varble' and waited.

There's a hideous stomach drop when you google an old friend, and no entries turn up: an absence that tells you this person had stopped existing by the time the web came along.

I tried again, and this time found a reference to 'the now forgotten performance artist Stephen Varble, an early Aids victim'. His dates: 1946–1984.

The knowledge that I'd stayed away from my friend when he was sick and dying was terrible.

But Stephen Varble *isn't* forgotten.

Over the next few months, I keep trawling, and finally a live item surfaces: David Getsy, a professor at the School of the Art Institute of Chicago, is doing research on Stephen Varble and genderqueer performance in the seventies. He's giving lectures, organizing an exhibition. I contact Getsy. The material record is scarce, he tells me: Stephen's last surviving costume, which had been stored in a friend's basement, was destroyed in Hurricane Sandy. I unearth my long-buried trove of Varble memorabilia, send Getsy scans of letters, photos, homemade press releases; Getsy mails me two stills from my vanished film with Stephen.

In May 2017, I go to Getsy's lecture on Varble and Genderqueer Street Performance at Queen Mary University in London, where I now live. Afterwards, the British graduate students debate whether Varble's geisha-girl motifs are orientalism, or a camp 'elevation of the racially downgraded other', and Getsy gently reminds them that Varble's art is not just critique, but also alive with 'disruptive pleasure'.

Today, radical art from the seventies and eighties, with its ethic of transience, marginality, inclusion of the excluded, looks 'right' to us. There are museum retrospectives of David Wojnarowicz, Peter Hujar, Adrian Piper; a new generation is discovering the work of Martin Wong, Klaus Nomi, the Cockettes, seeking out these crazily gifted artists and guerrilla performers whose exploration of gender transgression, socioeconomic precarity, institutional sexism and racism seem so prescient.

Stephen Varble, long forgotten, has finally come into his own. His playful assaults on museums, banks and luxury stores, wearing female-gendered garbage, now look totally on the mark.

In September, David Getsy's *Rubbish and Dreams* – the first exhibit of Varble's work since 1977 – will be opening at the Leslie-Lohman Museum of Gay and Lesbian Art on Wooster Street.

In April 1975, three weeks after our first encounter, I invited Stephen home to meet my parents. My parents were a curious mix: they hung out with underground filmmakers, but they were also Park Avenue society people, which meant that certain class boundaries had to be reinforced, terms negotiated, before their fourteen-year-old daughter could bring home the drag queen she'd met at the Easter Parade.

No, Stephen was not allowed to come to dinner, but he could come for an after-dinner drink. No, Stephen was not allowed to come as Marie Debris, but he could come in his civvies. This one almost proved a deal-breaker – Stephen claimed it was like 'asking a peacock to wear a raincoat', but in the end he appeared wearing jeans, an undershirt and full makeup.

'We had all been very tense, but it was alright, actually,' I noted in my diary. Stephen drank 'lots and lots of sherry', and he and my parents talked about Warhol stars they knew.

At midnight, my parents went to bed, and I fed Stephen the remains of the shad-roe dinner (Christ, if I could go back in time the first thing I'd do is make sure the boy got properly *fed*). We then dressed up in my mother's old clothes – Stephen in an emerald-green ostrich-feather jacket; me in an ankle-length Yves Saint Laurent cavalry coat – and headed down to a nightspot called Lady Astor's, on Lafayette Street.

> I had some allowance so I paid for everything. It was a quite weird, faintly congenial scene there – men in pink satin boots to their thighs. We sat on a crowded little sofa, talking about killing ourselves and Dostoevsky and Stephen's money problems. He is very desperate and unhappy. He feels that I don't like Marie Debris and said, 'I'm sorry, but I just can't give her up.

We drew a lot of stares, I noted, 'despite the unusual nature of the company'. After a few drinks – vodka gimlets for me, gin and tonics for him – Stephen cheered up:

> . . . so we left at about one thirty or quarter of two. The air was very cool and everyone we met was drunk, even the cats looked drunk. Stephen said that he had become obsessed by me and I was the one person in his life now . . . Stephen said he wanted to show me his favorite place in NYC. We went to this waterfront, under things which looked like an El [train tracks] fallen into desuetude and past this gay bar called something like Keller's. All these leather creatures were in front of it staring at us as we passed. It was the trucking district, there were thousands of trucks along these streets. We walked out to the river and squeezed in between trucks to this very spooky place, just the embankment by a pier very close to the murky water. The whole place was very deathly, S. said he came here sometimes when he thought of killing himself. I felt very spooked and also quite fascinated. S. is so brilliant – even Dad, who is not too astute about these things,

saw it. He needs a love object and I don't want it to be me, though it could become so despite what he refers to [as] his 'dubious orientation'. I only want to be what I am at present – a loved one, as he put it. We walked along the embankment, frequently running into sinister couples. I was the only woman I saw the whole time. We went out on the pier and passed this immense empty shell of a building about five floors and doorless. A few men entered it surreptitiously. It looked completely black inside. Stephen said it was the most exquisite place inside and very bizarre sex scenes went on in there – he wished he could take me in there but he was scared to, maybe we could come back. We went on for blocks and blocks, past tons of gay bars. He pointed out West Beth and we went into this discotheque for a few minutes inside an old warehouse. There were blocks of slaughterhouses which looked like deserted stables which had big signs which had words like 'feet flanks' on them. There were also 2 whorehouses, side by side, which people were filing into. They had hand-painted signs: THE STING and THE DUNGEON. The windows were cemented over. We spent until about 3.30 around there, talking very seriously. I wish he didn't need such constant reassuring and support, but . . . I feel good because there is certainty and security in our friendship.

Over the next couple of years, I kept returning to the West Side piers with Stephen. He'd dress me in his motorcycle jacket, and we'd cruise the S&M bars. I can still see the poster in the Eagle's Nest that said WEDNESDAY NIGHT FFA (Fist Fuckers of America), the swinging doors leading, I was told, to the 'dentist's chair with no seat to it'. (I never ventured farther than the front room.) I can still see the mustachioed men with their leather chaps and chains, leaning against a wall or pillar silent, unsmiling. How many of those men are alive today? I can still feel the charge of being in this intensely forbidden and forbidding environment, in which I was invisible and hence free to stare. Stephen used to worry that he'd get in trouble for bringing me, a female child, and no wonder, but the only 'trouble' was the night we got ambushed by one of the white gangs that came over from New Jersey or Little Italy to beat up gay men.

> Stephen giggled at the hurled bottles. 'Now you boys stop it before I lose my temper,' he threatened when they pulled to shreds his green ostrich feather bolero jacket.

This was a person who risked physical violence every time he set foot out of doors.

Forty-three years later, I'm thinking back to my nocturnal waterfront wanderings with Stephen. 1975 was the year when artist Gordon Matta-Clark created his site-specific *Day's End* in a rotting warehouse on the West Side piers – an area Matta-Clark described in oddly police-chief-like terms as housing 'a criminal situation of alarming proportions'. 1975 was when Peter Hujar, Leonard Fink and Alvin Baltrop first began photographing this post-industrial wasteland where, as Baltrop recalled, 'merrymaking . . . habitually gave way to muggings, callous yet detached violence, rape, suicide and, in some instances, murder'.

What was a fourteen-year-old girl doing on the West Side Highway at 3 a.m. with a transvestite who was dressed in her mother's clothes? Why did this desolate place seem, as I write in my diary, 'my promised land'? I survived my chronic taste for danger because I was privileged, white, female and lucky.

But many of my friends weren't so lucky, Stephen among them, and of all the artists and photographers I've mentioned, only one is still alive, Adrian Piper, which is why this piece is also a kind of 'Lament for the Makers'.

Partial List of Items in Stephen Varble's costumes:

Chicken bones
Milk cartons
A baby bottle
Piano keys
A head of lettuce
A typewriter ribbon
An air-conditioner insulator belt
A loaf of Wonder Bread
A toy fighter plane (worn as codpiece)
35 mm slides of his married lover's family vacations
(borrowed – and ruined – without permission)

After Getsy's lecture at Queen Mary University, he comes over to my place for dinner. I ask him about Stephen's final years. In the early eighties, Stephen and Daniel Cahill, the married merchant marine who was Stephen's last partner, became increasingly immersed in a religious cult of their own invention, holing up in their apartment on Riverside and 100th Street, and producing illuminated art and an unfinished video epic of a Pre-Raphaelite opulence and intricacy.

Earlier, I'd asked Getsy about Stephen's death. It was too sad, too disturbing, he'd said. He didn't want to spoil our evening. Now, choking up, he tells me what he's learned. After Stephen died, Cahill refused to let go of his body for days. Eventually, Cahill's wife had to get the fire department to break down the door and take Stephen's body away.

We sit in silence. Finally I say I don't think it's so sad; I think it's wonderful that Stephen died at home, so cherished. I think he would have seen such necrophiliac mourning as a refusal to submit to the 'strang unmercifull tyrand' who, as the sixteenth-century poet William Dunbar writes in his plague-time 'Lament for the Makers', was devouring his brightest peers.

Later, I learn that the person who told Getsy this story got it confused with someone else's death, and that actually Stephen died at Lenox Hill Hospital. In fact, very few people who died of an Aids-related illness, no matter how devoted their lovers, friends, family, or how much they loathed the state medical establishment's criminal indifference, was spared a hospital death, but it strikes me that there is nonetheless a kind of allegorical truth to the story.

For the last couple of years, I've been transcribing my diaries from the 1970s. Rereading them, I've felt haunted by Stephen's ghost. I can smell the metallic tinge of his perfume that reminded me of wire coat hangers, hear his mock-scandalized Kentucky intonations, touch the red-gold stubble on his chiseled chin. This ghost is demanding my recognition; our past is tangible.

We're *there*, on a mattress in the rubble-strewn basement of his patron Morihito Miyazaki's never-to-be-opened nightclub in the East 50s. It's 6 May 1976, 1.30 a.m. Stephen tries to make me eat a dead fly; I sing him my favorite Cole Porter song, 'I'm a Gigolo'; he bites my sneaker. We're trying to guess how many men Stephen's been to bed with – thousands – and I'm trying not to admit I haven't been to bed with any, and when he asks me who I fancy, I say Peter Hujar, and he threatens to call Peter and tell him to come right away.

> I kept saying I had to go, & Stephen kept giving reasons why I couldn't possibly. He was very piteous, because he had a bad cold, & of course is such a hypochondriac. He kept complaining about it, & my lack of sympathy & so finally I asked, rather annoyed, 'Well, what do you want me to do about it?' He said, 'You know the answer.' I didn't. 'Well, suck my cock.' I didn't however, & we parted on very good terms.

We had a strong sense of place, but no sense of time. We didn't know what was coming. We didn't know that this age of freedom would be so brief, that six years later, in David Wojnarowicz's words, people would begin 'waking up with the diseases of small birds and mammals', and that politicians and clergymen would use the public-health crisis to re-criminalize sexual 'deviance' and that real-estate developers would use it to expedite the clearances that would turn New York's unsafe spaces into a glossy simulacrum of the urban experience.

Stephen Varble's artistic practice, which at the time I found kind of embarrassing and that now seems powerfully truthful, lasted a mere nine years.

It's an autumn evening, 1977 now, Stephen and I are in a booth at the Lexington Candy Shop on 83rd, splitting a Dusty Road sundae. We're both ravenous, but I'm broke and he only has four dollars. I'm interviewing him about his recent action at Tiffany's, we're laughing at the Buster Keatonesque finale in which he and the security guards trying to eject him got stuck going round and round in the revolving doors.

I ask him to define his beliefs, and Stephen leans back, eyelids lowered so you see the violet veins, and says, 'I believe in the purity of artifice and the grandeur of the gutter.'

And what do *I* believe?

I'm asking myself this question today. I'm twenty years older than Stephen Varble was when he died, almost thirty years older than he was when we first met, and my answer is, I believe in him. ∎

Fernanda Eberstadt, two months before she met Stephen Varble, 1975
Courtesy of the author

Young Mennonite women, Durango, Mexico, 1994
© LARRY TOWELL / MAGNUM PHOTOS

Mennonites, Chihuahua, Mexico, 1996
© LARRY TOWELL / MAGNUM PHOTOS

WOMEN TALKING

Miriam Toews

Between 2005 and 2009, in a remote Mennonite colony in Bolivia (named the Manitoba Colony, after the province in Canada from which the colonists had emigrated in the mid-1900s), hundreds of girls and women would wake up in the morning feeling drowsy and in pain, their bodies bruised and bleeding, having been attacked in the night. The attacks were attributed to ghosts and demons. Some members of the community felt the women were being made to suffer by God or Satan as punishment for their sins; many accused the women of lying for attention or to cover up adultery; still others believed everything was the result of wild, female imagination. Eventually, it was revealed that eight men from the colony had been using an animal anaesthetic to knock their victims unconscious and rape them. In 2011, these men were convicted in a Bolivian court and received lengthy prison sentences. However, in 2013, while the convicted men were still in jail, it was reported that similar assaults and other sexual abuses were continuing to take place in the colony. What follows is fiction.

We begin by washing each other's feet. This takes time. We each wash the feet of the person sitting to our right. The foot-washing was a suggestion made by Agata Friesen (mother of Ona and Salome Friesen). It would be an appropriate symbolic act representing our service to each other, she said, just as Jesus washed the feet of his disciples at the Last Supper, knowing that his hour had come.

Four of the eight women are wearing plastic sandals with white socks, two are wearing sturdy leather shoes, scuffed (and in one case slit open at the side to allow for a growing bunion), with white socks, and the other two, the youngest, are wearing torn canvas running shoes, also with white socks. Socks are always worn by the women of Molotschna, and it appears to be a rule that the top of the socks must always reach the bottom hem of the dress.

The two youngest women, Autje and Neitje, the ones wearing running shoes, have rolled their socks down rebelliously (and stylishly) into little doughnuts that encircle their ankles. On them, a swatch of bare skin, several inches of skin, is visible between the rolled sock and the dress hem, and insect bites (probably black fly and chigger) dot the skin. Faint scars, from rope burns or from cuts, are also visible on the exposed parts of these women. Autje and Neitje, both sixteen, are having difficulty keeping straight faces during the foot-washing, murmuring to each other that it's ticklish, and coming close to erupting in giggles when attempting to say *God bless you* to each other, in solemn voices, as their mothers, aunts and grandmothers have done following each washing.

G reta Loewen, the eldest of the Loewen women (although she was born a Penner) begins. She exudes a deep, melancholic dignity as she speaks of her horses, Ruth and Cheryl. She describes how when Ruth (who is blind in one eye and must always be harnessed to the left of Cheryl) and Cheryl are frightened by one or more of Dueck's Rottweilers on the mile road that leads to church, their initial instinct is to bolt.

We have seen it happen, she says. (After these short, declarative sentences Greta has a habit of lifting her arms, dipping her head and widening her eyes as if to say, This is a fact, are you challenging me?)

Greta explains that these horses, upon being startled by Dueck's stupid dog, don't organize meetings to determine their next course of action. They run. And by so doing, evade the dog and potential harm.

Agata Friesen, the eldest of the Friesen women (although born a Loewen) laughs, as she does frequently and charmingly, and agrees. But Greta, she states, we are not animals.

Greta replies that we have been preyed upon like animals; perhaps we should respond in kind.

Do you mean we should run away? asks Ona.

Or kill our attackers? asks Salome.

(Mariche, Greta's eldest, until now silent, makes a soft scoffing sound.)

Agata Friesen, unfazed by Salome's outbursts (she has already referred to Ecclesiastes to describe Salome's temper as nothing new under the sun, as the wind blows from the north, as all streams lead to the sea, etc. To which Salome responded that her opinions should not be slotted under hoary Old Testament headings, please, and wasn't it preposterous that the women should compare themselves to animals, wind, sea, etc? Isn't there a human precedent, some person in whom we can see ourselves reflected back to ourselves? To which Mejal, lighting up a smoke, responded, Yes, I'd like that, too, but what humans? Where?), states that in her lifetime she has seen horses, perhaps not Ruth or Cheryl, fair enough – in deference to Greta and her high regard for her horses – but others who, when charged by a dog or coyote or jaguar, have attempted to confront the animal and/or to stomp the creature to death. So it isn't always the case that animals flee their attackers.

Greta acknowledges this: yes, she has seen similar behaviour in animals. She begins once again to talk of Ruth and Cheryl, but her anecdote is cut short by Agata.

Agata tells the group she has her own animal story, also featuring Dueck's Rottweiler. She speaks quickly, often inserting asides and non sequiturs in a hushed, theatrical voice.

I am not able to hear or keep up with every detail, but I'll attempt here to tell the story in her voice, and with as much accuracy as I am able.

Dueck had raccoons in his yard that he hated for a long time, and when the fattest raccoon suddenly had six babies, it was all that Dueck could stand. He tore his hair out. He told his Rottweiler to go kill them, and away the dog went, and the mother raccoon was surprised and tried to save her babies and get away from the dog, but the dog killed three of the babies and the mother raccoon could only save the other three. She took those babies and left Dueck's yard. Dueck was fairly happy about that. He drank his instant coffee, and thought, praise be to God, no more raccoons. But a few days later, he looked into his yard and saw the three baby raccoons sitting there, and he became angry once again. He told his Rottweiler again to attack and kill them. But this time the mother raccoon was waiting for the dog, and when he came running at the babies she jumped on him from a tree and bit into his neck and his stomach and then, with every muscle in her body straining, dragged him into the bushes. Dueck was so mad, and also sad. He wanted his dog back. He went into the bushes to find the dog, but he couldn't, even after two days of searching. He cried. When he came back home he walked despondently to his door and there lay one leg from his dog, and also the dog's head. With empty eye sockets.

The reaction to Agata's story is mixed. Greta lifts her hands over her head and asks the other women: What are we supposed to make of this? Are we to leave our most vulnerable colony members exposed to further attack in order to lure the men to their deaths so they can be dismembered and delivered in parts to the doorstep of Peters, the bishop of our colony?

What the story proves is that animals can fight back *and* they can run away, Agata says. And so it doesn't matter whether we are animals or not, or whether we have been treated like animals or not, or even if we can know the answer to that one way or the other. (She inhales all possible oxygen into her lungs and then releases it with the next sentence.) Either way, it's a waste of time to try to establish whether we are animals or not, when the men will soon be returning from the city.

Mariche Loewen raises her hand. One of her fingers, her left index, has been bitten off at the knuckle. It is half as long as the middle finger next to it. She asserts that in her opinion, the more important question to ask is not whether the women are animals, but rather, should the women avenge the harm perpetrated against them? Or should they instead forgive the men and by doing so be allowed to enter the gates of Heaven? We will be forced to leave the colony, she says, if we don't forgive the men and/or accept their apologies, and through the process of this excommunication we will forfeit our place in Heaven. (Note: this is true, I know, according to the rules of Molotschna.)

Mariche sees me looking at her and asks if I'm writing this down. I nod, yes, I am.

Satisfied, Mariche asks the others a question about the rapture. How will the Lord, when He arrives, find all the women if we aren't in Molotschna?

Salome cuts her off, disdainful. In a mocking voice, she begins to explain that if Jesus is able to return to life, live for thousands of years and then drop down to earth from heaven to scoop up his supporters, surely he'd also be able to locate a few women who –

But now Salome is silenced by her mother, Agata, with a quick gesture. We will return to that question later, Agata says kindly.

Mariche's eyes dart around the room, perhaps searching for kinship on this subject, someone to share her fears. The others look away.

Salome is muttering: But if we're animals, or even animal-like, perhaps there's no chance anyway of entering the gates of Heaven – (she stands up and goes to the window) – unless animals are permitted. Although that doesn't make sense because animals provide food and labour, and we will require neither of those things in Heaven. So perhaps, after all, Mennonite women will not be allowed into heaven because we fall into the category of animals, who will not be needed up there, where it's always *lalalalala* . . . She ends her sentence in song syllables.

The other women, except Ona Friesen, her sister, ignore her. Ona smiles slightly, encouragingly, approvingly, although it's also a smile that could serve as firm punctuation to Salome's statement – that is, a silent request to end it. (The Friesen women have developed a mostly effective system of gestures and facial expressions to quiet Salome.)

Ona begins to speak now. She is reminded of a dream she had two nights ago: she found a hard candy in the dirt behind her home and had picked it up and taken it into her kitchen, planning to wash it and eat it. Before she could wash it, she was accosted by a very large 200-pound pig. She screamed, Get that pig off me! But it had her pinned against the wall.

That's ridiculous, says Mariche. We don't have hard candy in Molotschna.

Agata reaches over to touch Ona's hand. You can tell us your dreams later, she says. When the meeting is over.

Several of the women speak up now, saying they are not able to forgive the men.

Precisely, says Mariche. She speaks succinctly, sure of herself again. Yet we want to enter the gates of Heaven when we die.

None of the women argue that point.

Mariche goes on to state that we should then not put ourselves in an unfortunate position, where we are forced to choose between forgiveness and eternal life.

What position would that be? asks Ona Friesen.

That position would be staying behind to fight, Mariche says. Because the fight would be lost to the men, and we would be guilty of the sin of rebellion and of betraying our vow of pacifism and would finally be plunged deeper into submissiveness and vulnerability. Furthermore, we would be forced to forgive the men anyway, if we wanted God to forgive us and to allow us into His kingdom.

But is forgiveness that is coerced true forgiveness? asks Ona Friesen. And isn't the lie of pretending to forgive with words but not with one's heart a more grievous sin than to simply not forgive? Can't there be a category of forgiveness that is up to God alone, a category that includes the perpetration of violence upon one's children, an act so impossible for a parent to forgive that God, in His wisdom, would take exclusively upon Himself the responsibility for such forgiveness?

Do you mean that God would allow the parent of the violated child to harbour just a tiny bit of hatred inside her heart? asks Salome. Just in order to survive?

A tiny bit of hate? asks Mejal. That's ridiculous. And from tiny seeds of hate bigger –

It's not ridiculous, says Salome. A very small amount of hate is a necessary ingredient to life.

To life? says Mejal. You mean to waging war. I've noticed how you come alive in the act of killing.

Salome rolls her eyes. Not war; survival. And let's not call it hate –

Oh, you'd prefer to call it an 'ingredient', says Mejal.

When I must kill pigs, I hit the runts harder, says Salome, because it's more humane to kill them with one swift blow than to torture them with tepid hacks, which your system . . .

I wasn't talking about killing pigs, says Mejal.

During this exchange, Mejal's daughter Autje has begun swinging from a rafter, a human pendulum, kicking at bales mid-swing and loosening the straw, a piece of which has landed in Salome's hair. Mejal looks up, tells Autje to behave herself, can't she hear the rafter creaking, does she want the roof to cave in? (I muse that perhaps she does.)

Mejal reaches for her pouch of tobacco but doesn't roll a smoke, simply rests her hand lightly on the pouch as though it were a gear shift in an idling getaway car, and she is waiting, knowing it is there when she needs it because her hand is on it.

Salome doesn't know about the straw in her hair. It sits above her ear, nestled in that space, like a librarian's No. 2 pencil.

After a small silence, Greta returns to Ona's question. Perhaps, yes, such a category exists, she says slowly. Except there's no biblical precedent for this type of God-only forgiveness.

MIRIAM TOEWS

A brief observation about Ona Friesen: Ona is distinctive among these women for having her hair pulled back loosely rather than with the blunt force of a seemingly primitive tool. She is perceived by most of the colonists to have a gentle disposition and an inability to function in the real world (although in Molotschna that argument is a red herring). She is a spinster. And she is afforded a type of liberty to speak her mind because her thoughts and words are perceived as meaningless, although this didn't prevent her from being attacked repeatedly. She was a reliable target because she slept alone in a room rather than with a husband, which she doesn't have. Or want, it seems.

Earlier she had stated: When we have liberated ourselves, we will have to ask ourselves who we are. Now she asks: Is it accurate to say that at this moment we women are asking ourselves what our priority is, and what is right – to protect our children or to enter the kingdom of Heaven?

Mejal Loewen says, No. That is not accurate. That is an exaggeration of what is truly being discussed. (Her hand still resting intimately on the pouch of tobacco.)

What, then, is truly being discussed? Ona asks.

Agata Friesen, Ona's mother (and Mejal's aunt), responds. We will burn that bridge when we come to it, she says (intentionally using this English expression incorrectly in order to leaven the proceedings). And Ona, indulgent of her mother, as she is of her sister, is content to let it be.

Greta Loewen pats Autje's hand. *Steady on.* The knuckles on Greta's hand stand out like knobs, like desert buttes on a cracked surface. Her false teeth are too big for her mouth, and painful. She removes them and sets them down on the plywood. They were given to her by a well-meaning traveller who had come to Molotschna with a first aid kit after hearing about the attacks on the women.

When Greta had cried out, the attacker covered her mouth with such force that nearly all her teeth, which were old and fragile, were crushed to dust. The traveller who gave Greta her false teeth was escorted out of Molotschna by Peters, who then forbade outside helpers from entering the colony.

The singing has ended. The women disperse.

Note: Salome Friesen left earlier, exasperated, after Ona asked if the women were discussing what was right, to protect the children or to enter the kingdom of Heaven, and if it wasn't possible to do both. I hadn't the time then to write down the details of her departure.

Salome's youngest daughter, Miep, was violated by the men on two or possibly three different occasions, but Peters denied medical treatment for Miep, who is three years of age, on the grounds that the doctor would gossip about the colony and that people would become aware of the attacks and the whole incident would be blown out of proportion. Salome walked twelve miles to the next colony to procure antibiotics for Miep from the Mobile Klinic that she knew was stationed there, temporarily, for repairs. (And to pick up moonshine for herself, according to Mariche, who on several occasions when Salome is raging has indicated, by miming the act of bringing a bottle to her mouth, that Salome secretly drinks.)

I have to hide the antibiotics in Miep's strained beets or she won't swallow them, says Salome.

The women nod and tell her to go, go.

As she leaves, Salome suggests that if Mejal goes to get the soup from the summer kitchen then Salome could bring the spelt bread she baked this morning. We will all have this food for lunch, Salome says, and continue with our meeting as we eat. We will have instant coffee.

Mejal shrugs, languidly – she hates to be told what to do by Salome – but rises from her chair.

Agata, meanwhile, remains perfectly still, mouthing the words to a prayer or a verse, perhaps one from Psalms. Miep is her granddaughter, named after her. ('Miep' is a nickname.) Agata is a strong woman but whenever she hears the specific details of the attack on her tiny granddaughter she becomes very still, predatory.

(When Salome discovered that Miep had been attacked not once but two or three times, she went to the shed where the men were being kept and attempted to kill them all with a scythe. This was the incident that convinced Peters to call the police and have the men arrested and brought to the city where they would be safe. Salome claims she did ask to be forgiven for that outburst, and that the men forgave her, but nobody, including Peters, witnessed this. Perhaps these last facts are not germane to the minutes of the meetings but I believe they're significant enough to include in the footnotes because without the perpetrators having been taken to the city, and the other men of the colony following them to post bail in order to have them returned to the colony, where they could be forgiven by the victims and in turn have the victims forgiven by God, these meetings would not be happening.)

The Lord is gracious and compassionate, slow to anger, rich in loving kindness and forgiving, says Agata.

She repeats this, and Greta takes Agata's hand and joins her in the recitation.

Mejal Loewen has left the room, I presume to smoke, even though she has declared that she is going to get the soup from the summer kitchen. She ordered Autje, her daughter, not to follow her, and Autje made a face as if to say, Why would I bother? And also a face to the others, as if to apologize for her strange mother, the smoker with the secret life.

Miep and the other little children from the colony are being looked after by several young women at the home of Nettie Gerbrandt, whose husband is away in the city with the others. Nettie Gerbrandt's twin brother, Johan, is one of the eight on trial. Miep herself is unaware of why she experiences pain in certain parts of her small body, or that she has a sexually transmitted illness. Nettie Gerbrandt, too, was attacked, possibly by her brother, and gave birth prematurely to a baby boy so tiny he fit into her shoe. He died hours after being born and Nettie smeared her bedroom walls with blood. She has stopped talking, except to the children of the colony, which is why she has been put in charge of their care while the others work.

Mariche Loewen believes that Nettie may have changed her name to Melvin. She believes Nettie has done this because she no longer wants to be a woman. Agata and Greta refuse to believe this.

I ask for a quick breather.

Ona Friesen once again glances at me inquisitively – or perhaps she is curious at the notion of a 'breather' (which, likely, is not a word she has ever heard before, even in translation), or at the notion of the sustained breath, the exquisite agony of the unexpressed thought, the narrative of life, the thread that binds, that knots, that holds. A breather, breath, sustained. The narrative.

The women give me their consent.

The women settle in for more discussion. Shadows fall on their faces and upon the piece of plywood set up to be their table. I have spotted several mice – or is it the same mouse, an exceptionally active one? Autje and Neitje, still comically conjoined, are using their kerchiefs to swipe at flies.

(Technically these kerchiefs are to be worn by all women over the age of fifteen in the presence of men. I have never seen Autje's and Neitje's hair before. It looks very soft – blonde in the case of Neitje, with varying shades from nearly white to golden to beige, and in the case of Autje, dark brown with a discreet auburn glaze, a colour that matches her eyes and also the manes and tails of Ruth and Cheryl, Greta's skittish team. I am ashamed to admit that I wonder if Autje and Neitje do not consider me enough of a man, or really one at all, to warrant covering their hair in my presence.)

Agata is barefoot now. She raises her legs and props them on a piece of wood to reduce the fluid build-up she suffers from. Oedema, she calls it. There is a note of pride in her voice when she says the word 'oedema'. (There must be satisfaction gained in accurately naming the thing that torments you.)

Salome has laid Miep down on a saddle blanket beside her, and the child is the focal point of the assembled women.

Agata has asked me to print in large letters:

OPTIONS FOR THE MEN AND OLDER BOYS IF THE WOMEN DECIDE TO LEAVE

1. That they be allowed to leave with the women if they wish.
2. That they be allowed to leave with the women only if they sign the declaration/manifesto.
3. That they be left behind.
4. That they be allowed to join the women later, when the women have determined where they're going and have established themselves and are thriving as a democratic/collective/literate community (with progress reports made regularly on the rehabilitation/behaviour of the men and boys with regard to the women and girls).

NB: Boys under the age of twelve, simple-minded boys of any age, Cornelius (a colony boy of fifteen who is confined to a wheelchair) and the elderly/infirm men who are unable to care for themselves (these are the boys and men who have remained here instead of going to the city) will automatically accompany the women.

For the first time since the commencement of the meeting, the women appear to be genuinely perplexed. They are silent, deep in thought.

Mariche speaks first. She votes for the first option.

This sits well with no one else. Voices are raised in unison and Mariche crosses her arms. She is anxious to leave. She tosses the dregs of her instant coffee onto the floor, says she'd like to strangle herself.

But Mariche, says Ona, the possibility arises of the men, perhaps all of them, choosing to leave with us, and all we'd be doing is recreating our existing colony, with all of its inherent dangers, elsewhere, wherever we end up.

Agata adds: And the men would most definitely leave with us because they can't survive without us.

Greta laughs and says, Well, not for longer than a day or two.

Salome points out that option number one is really rather moot. If we do decide ultimately to leave the colony rather than to stay and fight, she says, we will leave the colony before the men return, so there is no possibility of the men leaving *with* us.

Mejal, now openly smoking (although, because it vexes Salome, making grand gestures of batting the smoke away from sleeping Miep), states that option number one is ridiculous and should be scratched off the list. She further states that option number two (allowing the men to leave with the women if the men sign the manifesto of demands) is, for the same reason as number one, moot. Furthermore, says Mejal, even if we did decide to leave only after the men have returned, and to take with us those of the men who agree to sign the manifesto, how do we know that their acts of signing are not treacherous? Who, other than the women of Molotschna, could be more aware of the duplicity of men?

Well spoken, says Ona.

Mariche states: Well then, let's be done with it and leave the men behind. Number three it is! She slams the table (plywood) with her fist, and Miep stirs.

Salome asks Mariche to restrain herself.

O na's voice is all we/I hear. She is playful as she sings, speeding up the lyrics as the fish winnow and race, slowing them down as the fish bask in the sunlight close to the surface of the water. The children are calm, enthralled. Ona continues to sing the song about ducks swimming in the sea, one, two, three and four.

Ona asks the children if they know what a sea is, and they stare at her with four enormous blue eyes, sea-like. Ona describes the sea as another world, one that is hidden from us, one that lives underwater. It is the life in the sea that she defines as the sea, and not the sea itself. She talks about fish and other living things.

At last, Mariche interrupts. The sea is a vast expanse of water, and nothing else, she tells the children. They're children, Ona, she explains. How can they be expected to understand what goes on invisibly? Besides, you have never seen a sea.

Salome begins to laugh. She says: The life underwater is not invisible. It isn't unable to be seen. We just can't see it from here. My God.

You are ignorant of a child's sensibilities, Salome, says Mariche.

Oh, says Salome, am I? If I allowed my child to be beaten black and blue by a shit for brains, like your Klaas, would I be considered less ignorant of how a child perceives a hidden life?

Mariche is silent, shocked.

Salome, says Mejal, that doesn't make any sense. She advises Salome to have a drag from her cigarette.

Ona agrees, silently. I know that she thinks Salome's attack was unclear and beneath her. I know it because she looked at Salome and furrowed her brow in a way that I witnessed earlier (the disappearing rail tracks that line her forehead). Overall, Ona is tolerant of her sister's rages and circumspect in her response to them. Perhaps she has learned over the years that no good comes from crossing her younger sibling.

As if reading my thoughts, Agata now suggests that we *think* of what is good. She recites a verse from Philippians: Whatever is true, whatever is honourable, whatever is just, whatever is pure, whatever is lovely, whatever is commendable, if there is any excellence and if there is anything worthy of praise, think about these things . . . and the peace of God be with you.

The other women wait for each other to speak first, to answer Agata's call for suggestions of goodness. In truth, the women seem not to be actively engaged in this endeavour.

Salome bypasses the question altogether. I will become a murderer if I stay, she says to her mother. (I assume that she means if she stays in the colony, and is here when and if the captured men are granted bail and return home from the city.)

What is worse than that? Salome asks Agata. ■

Paris Hilton

ON PARIS HILTON AND OTHER UNDEAD THINGS

Brittany Newell

It will come back to haunt you.

This is the keystone threat of the digital age. It's the threat used to dissuade girls from doing porn. 'What if your kids see it?' my mother screamed when I briefly considered posing for *Playboy*. It's the threat leveled at teen sexters, oversharing vloggers, anyone with a thirst trap Instagram. *Be careful what you put out there*, people warn, as if you were a camper putting out food scraps for bears. *These things might come back to haunt you.*

Rhetorically, it's a curious phrase. It is a threat suggesting the undeadness of digital images, their lack of mooring to one time or place. Like Irish ghosts, they roam forever. Off-screen, it is the threat of climate change and its slow ravages, of individual actions in a globalized world, of gossip and cigarettes – that first drag will haunt you. It is also, on a scale both private and global, spanning hard drive to market to ether, the threat of the sex tape.

The threat evokes the rapid speed of transmission and circularity that defines internet porn, and has made sex tapes like *1 Night in Paris* the stuff of sleepover lore – indeed, the eerie use of night vision makes that tape's ghostliness explicit. It is a threat concerned with both the future and the past, pitting the soon-to-be-past you (so craaazy) against the distant-future you (with a reputation, with kids). On an affective level, it is a threat invoking memory, that which we will be haunted by no matter how wild or mild our escapades. At twenty-three I am haunted by the memory of far less sensational things my body has done, on- and off-camera. I still remember the video-rental store I used to go to as a kid: Silver Screen, smack dab in the center of a dying strip mall. I'm haunted by its plastic smell, its inch-thick carpet and the red velvet curtain in the back, with a sign that said 18+ ONLY. I never got to see what was behind the red curtain; by the time I was old enough, the store was long gone.

These things might come back to haunt you.

Yet for all its force, the threat is unclear. Who or what carries out this haunting? Is it the younger you in the sex tape, the body made foreign by grainy reproduction and an outdated belly ring? Will this body haunt the distant-future you with her youth, her ease, with embarrassing noises you've since learned not to make? Or is it the video itself that does the haunting, the redirect to porn sites that haunts all future Google searches for your name? Is the sex tape ghostly because it follows you around, like a stigma, or because you can't touch its bodies, no matter how real they seem?

Or vaguer still, is it the mere knowledge of the sex tape's existence that will haunt you? Like, even if you never see the tape again, you will be kept awake by the suspicion that somewhere, through the time warp of cyberspace, a zitty citizen might be watching you get off, nursing a semi as he clicks other links. This audience of one will haunt you; you, with your belly ring, might haunt him.

I live in San Francisco, a city haunted by missions, Aids and the fog. I agree with the songs that say people are gentler here, more submissive to the flux. We lie down in our parks and close our bars early. People with money theorize utopia, drink fresh-pressed juice. Things have always had the shimmer of the too-good-to-be-true. As new technologies make the body feel diffuse (which can be sexy) and irrelevant (which can be grim), I find myself seeking spaces or zones in which I feel contained. These need not be brick-and-mortar locations. If all that is solid melts into air and the Amazon superstores are run entirely by bots, it would seem physicality is a moot point; what matters most in the drone age is faith. As Philip Rosedale, founder of the San Francisco lab behind *Second Life*, says, 'Things are real because they're there with us and we believe in them.'

It is this faith in the nonmaterial that unites the poet and the gamer, the psychic and the techie, as they reject the flesh in favor of signs, be they Foucauldian or paranormal. One need not have a body in order to be touched: this concept has long gone mainstream, and makes sense to anyone who texts and thus understands the gravity of the red-rose emoji. This renunciation of matter can make you feel like a god (omnipresent) or a Popsicle (melting fast). Personally I'm OK with getting rid of my body; I see the appeal of newer, better containers. In a post-body landscape, I'm interested in where touch will take place. In our parks? In our contact lists? I'm interested in the spaces that exist within these so-called non-places.

What is a non-place? There are many ways to define the term, put forth by French anthropologist Marc Augé to describe 'a space which cannot be defined as relational, or historical, or concerned with identity'. A non-place is somewhere my architect father, always snooty about vibes, might call 'soulless', like a big-chain multiplex with fluorescent lights, inexplicably decorated in oranges and tans. The strip mall that once housed Silver Screen, alongside a bagel shop and a stationery store, was a non-place. An airport, with its sterile cheer, is the classic example: better yet, an airport bar, with its pseudo-European fixtures and French fries in a wire cone, its line of soft-bellied businessmen playing footsie and watching the game. Another example: the fast-growing condos in San Francisco's former meat market. The bars may shut at two in SF, but the gyms are twenty-four hours. Once I went all the way to the fifth floor of a Holiday Inn near Times Square only to learn, after fiddling with my keycard for ten minutes, that I was in the wrong hotel. *My* Holiday Inn was across the street.

Once armed with the term, one can see non-places everywhere. One might think of refugee camps. One might think of the Metaverse. One might think of endless bureaucratic hallways, or endless bureaucratic email chains. One might think of online shopping emporia like Amazon, which are literally malls located nowhere. One might think of the tense quiet of an Uber. One might think of the comments section on a political article, into which one is sucked for hours. I am attracted to these looser uses of the term, as 'non-place' morphs into a shorthand for the sense of unreality alleged to define our post-postmodern existence of half-truths and year-round avocados.

My questions are, when all the world becomes a waiting room, how does one preoccupy oneself? When the muzak plays, where does one dance?

Cut to my interest in amateur pornography, or, more sweetly put, the sex tape. There are those who say that you can learn everything you need to know about the twenty-first century from the Kardashians. Let's not forget, then, what started it all – the seed of their empire: Kim's sex tape.

I like the term 'sex tape' for its anachronistic conjuring of videotapes, things filmed on a camcorder and stuffed into the VCR: compact, discrete and holdable. Perhaps my nineties childhood has instilled in me a tenderness toward VHS, on a par with my attraction to hot pink and Kelly green. The phrase 'sex tape' feels directly opposed to the spacy feeling of non-places, evoking the material, hard shiny black plastic, long after the sex tape has morphed into a transnational tele-digital commodity. The speed with which sex tapes are transmitted, seen, copied and compressed speaks to the placeless network of relations that defines globalization. Sex tapes would seem to be a prime example of the body made commodity, a literalization of the late capitalist truism that there is nothing which is not market, including (or especially) shaky fellatio in motel lamplight.

I'm reminded of that stoner truism, that if you can think of a title for a porno, it must already exist. Long car rides have been passed in this fashion: *Withering Heights*! *Lord of the Cock Rings*! *My Big Fat Greek Penis*! My friend told me about a man she met on Grindr whose fantasy was to be small enough to fit in the palm of your hand. His username was, aptly, VerySmallMan. In her novella, dominatrix Reba Maybury describes a sub, nicknamed Humpty Dumpty, whose fantasy is being force-fed until he is so massive that he becomes a genderless blob. He illustrates this fantasy on his Tumblr with stock footage of tropical-print beanbags. He wants to get so big that a woman can comfortably recline on him.

Express yourself!!! the market bellows. Everything is up for grabs. And why not? Physicality is a moot point; sex is not an act but a headspace. We've all fucked Paris Hilton. A fantasy can be entered again and again, quietly, easily, in the non-place of one's choosing. In the loneliest of places, an airport bar or Hilton hotel room, you need not feel alone; you need not even feel human.

According to the logic of the non-place, to be in a Hilton hotel in Dallas is the same as to be in a Hilton hotel in Dubai or Dublin. Regarding *1 Night in Paris*, one might go so far as to say that to be in Paris Hilton is the same as to be in Paris, France, which is the same as to be in Paris, Texas. Fantasy fixates, and thus fixes the parameters, such that one knows where to go when one wants to feel good. One night in Paris becomes a lifetime supply, an unending season in Paris if that's your go-to happy place. One might recall Rosedale's statement: *things are real because they're with us and we believe in them.* Cue George Michael, a recent ghost: *you gotta have faith!* Or perhaps one recalls a song played in waiting rooms and airport bars the world over, a song that, for better or worse, will never die: *Plenty of room at the Hotel California . . . Any time of year, you find it here.* Which California is up to you.

Before I go further, let me say plainly: I love Paris Hilton. I think she is a prophet of the watched age, disarmingly sweet. I grew up seeing her name in every checkout aisle; I remember the FREE PARIS T-shirts after her arrest. She is responsible for so many of the things I associate with my pre-Y2K childhood: belly rings, tiny purses, tabloid fever and, come the 2000s, reality TV. *The Simple Life,* ethics aside, is an incredible document with regards to white privilege, self-surveillance, female intimacy and the American imagination. *The Simple Life* follows Paris and BFF Nicole as they bounce between non-places, sampling drab summer jobs at Burger Kings and Walmarts and factory farms. They get up to no good in windowless break rooms. Their bewilderment at the American landscape is meant to be funny, a consequence of their alienation as celebrities, but watching Paris get lost in the frozen-food aisle of a chain supermarket (*like, what makes it, like, super?*), I relate. She's the reason I wore my pants ultra-low, the reason I draw out my vowels and talk slow. She's been the ghost in my closet and throat since '02. She lingers in every 'like'.

Let's talk more about ghosts. Colin Davis neatly describes the concept of hauntology, coined in 1993 by Derrida: 'Hauntology supplants its near-homonym ontology, replacing the priority of being and presence with the figure of the ghost as that which is neither present nor absent, neither dead nor alive.' Say it again: *things are real because they're with us and we believe in them.*

What sex tapes offer, on a hauntological level, is an impossible closeness to that which is neither dead nor alive. The bodies in the tape are real, or used to be, but the threesome formed by your attention, your jollies, rewrites history. Perhaps this explains the specific kicks of watching a sex tape, the thrilling sense of infringement as one observes Paris flicking her belly ring. To watch a sex tape is to be aroused while simultaneously unsettled, to be an anthropologist and also a kid – nudging open closed doors, shocked by your findings.

In these televisual documents, one is presented with a frightfully candid world, replete with nonfictional objects like garbage and dogs, white noise, dirty linen, makeup strewn on the counter. The trash looks alive. Clutter becomes a signifier of authenticity, as does a certain distractibility. The camera can't focus. One is absorbed by the erotic action, yet never unaware of the device recording it, nor the video's status as just that.

'Is this thing on?' Paris asks. Within seconds, the fourth wall is broken, like a champagne glass.

'Ewwww!' she cries when the cameraman teases her. She shuts the door in his, our, face. By assuming his point of view, do we become him? Most people watching would probably rather be Paris.

Later, his off-screen voice teases: 'I thought you were a wild party girl! What happened to you?'

'I never was,' she whines. The bleariness of her reproduction, against the bland drapes of a midsized hotel room, makes this statement of nonbeing feel poignant and true.

Later still, the camera is set on a table. We watch it shift from side to side. Paris flops in a standard-issue armchair, spike heels on the bed. Everything in the room is the color of oatmeal. She points out a better position. 'Over there.' The cameraman, still unseen, suddenly a perfectionist, mutters: 'Actually, it looked better before.'

These unscripted moments in *1 Night* are gold. After all, it's not a regular porn film one has chosen to watch, but a sex tape: an artifact, whose status as real is underscored by its amateur aesthetic. This aesthetic includes shaky camerawork, off-screen breathing, jerky zooms, unflattering angles, mumbled asides and long, unedited, unpornographic interludes. The amateur (also called realcore) is a genre of porn defined by its claims to realism. The style swings from art film to *Planet Earth* documentary, MTV behind-the-scenes to *The Blair Witch Project*. The fantasy world one enters has more of the quality of memory, imperfect and banal, than cinema. Paris is hairless, but grainy. She is present, but low-res. She's not a poster, but a ghost.

Here is a genre perfectly suited to supermodernity, in which uncertainty and blurriness are understood as keystones of reality. In order to define the current moment, which some call post-postmodernity, some reach for examples of late capitalism at its most demented, of environmental destruction that crosses national lines, of AI and transhumanist propaganda. I reach for the sense of unreality relayed by Paris Hilton in black underwear: her real/digital/hyped body as the site where the viral and desirous collapse into one, an overdetermined symbol that can't be controlled. We own her; she, a billionaire, owns us. Paris zings through the ether at nonhuman speeds, but it's really *really* her you're seeing on your screen. The graininess is proof. Clarity and the absolute are rejected: in 2018, they are neither probable nor hot. All that is solid melts into air, and the amateur sex tape, echoing innumerable theorists, fetishizes this smeary state as the realest of real. Our babes are not airbrushed, but air brushing past.

It seems important to note that Derrida was conceptualizing hauntology in 1993, when hackers were sexy and the internet new:

a Baudrillardian moment of techno-tele-discursivity, Simulacra with a capital S, and hot pink. According to realcore expert Sergio Messina, the amateur fetish boom began in 1997–98 when digital photography first became popular. Digital cameras would help shape the sex tape in its evolution from cheeky Polaroid to in-group DVD to hacked celebrity file. Realcore fetishizes realism, but it is a special brand of real: the compromised realism of fragmented bodies in flux, of jump cuts and bad lighting, born of the digital age. Realcore prizes the uncanny, the creeping familiarity of piled towels and beige walls, of famous bodies bunched and bored in hotel suites. Enter the ghost, another instance of compromised realism: the body both real *and* phantasmic, familiar and freaky, the arresting figure not-all-there.

Paris Hilton herself alleged that she was not-all-there – in her words, 'out of it' – when *1 Night in Paris* was recorded. This claim triggered a defamation suit from then-boyfriend and substandard cameraman Rick Salomon. Watching the tape, I believe her. I understand how she could be both deeply in and out of it. Sex can be a non-place too. And it is precisely her semi-presence, not-all-there, that continues to circulate, on the internet and in the mind, as one recalls her baby voice and limp, long limbs. It is the sense that she's 'gone' in multiple senses that makes the tape so haunting.

What makes a sex tape signify as real are its ghostly qualities. The blurs, the shakes, the I-*think*-that's-what's-happening-there; the sense that physical bodies, once real in the classic sense, have been imperfectly conjured, and are now real in a different sense. 'You're, like, obsessed with filming me,' Paris tells the bodiless cameraman. Like a ghost, he flits in and out of visibility, appearing sporadically in a corner of the mirror, bulked up by white towels. His off-screen laughter and cokey commands – *say hello to my little friend!* – chase Paris as she moves away from, then toward, then away from the camera. But of course, in the parameters set by the fantasy and the duration of the tape, there is no escape.

This actually happened, the sex tape insists of its bodies, with their stretch marks and sad rooms. It is historical, yours to observe from the allegedly firm ground of the present. And yet, with a sort of techno-utopian exuberance, it also insists: *This can happen again, over and over, forever, for you!* Paris always squealing 'siiiick!' in any Hilton of your choosing. It is a fantasy: yours for the taking, yours to express yourself with, yours to spread over the internet and send to your friends, yours to go into whenever you'd like. The sex tape presents realism for those who know that nothing is real.

It will come back to haunt you: in 2018, this is not only the threat of the sex tape but also its promise.

Realcore pivots on this eerie return. Perhaps the naysayers are right: perhaps that sex tape will come back to haunt its eighteen-year-old star, her belly ring long since removed. But the threat goes both ways. The sex tape will haunt us too, as its viewers and inhabitants. It will house us, with its fantastic infrastructure. We were there, in that bedroom. We pulled aside the velvet curtain. The sex tape is a haunted house, or should I say, a haunted hotel, a haunted Hilton, in the spectral California dusk of a fixed 73 degrees. It could be in Hollywood, or San Francisco, or an anonymous rest area off CA-1. Take your pick. But beware the reggae-inflected threat: you can check out any time you wish (flash to Paris's out-of-it body, checked-out, not-all-there), but you can never leave. ∎

Momtaza Mehri

Though I Have Never Been to Ostia, I Have Seen the Place Where Our Dreams Died

like pasolini's dream of an african *oresteia*   let us be ridiculous

you will still be young like him in a bright shirt ashamed of the birds in your chest

suffused with the secret of wombs wanting to die before you are killed by something

tell me your first thought upon waking   not the second   not the rumor

the lewd perfume that laughs along innocent limbs in granulated detail   repeat after me

there is no such thing as a peaceful translation   dry-mouthed agitation   won't save you

neither will poetry   the pyramid scheme of revolution   not its child   nor changeling

faithless attentions   the dimpled chin of william o'neal   a joyriding teen   so scared

of nonbeing   of the lolling tongues of bars & guards he led them to fred hampton's bed *going mad*

then walked   twenty years later   straight into the eisenhower expressway   how tender

in the middle of this ordinary night how achingly black the sky must have been do they not betray

after a thousand other nights are the birds not informants too? do they not betray

each coming dawn? their *cruel indifference of glances*   their absolute fidelity

to nothing but themselves   & the bruised heavens heavens heavens

NOTE ON THE POEM: Italicised text from Pier Paolo Pasolini's poem 'Flesh and Sky', translated from the Italian by David Stivender and J.D. McClatchy.

the
personal
is
political!

TELLING MY STORY

Stella Duffy

There are muted voices in the #MeToo discussions, hushed, deleted. Too often these are the voices of poor women, women of colour, elderly women, of women who are still girls and not able to speak up yet, disabled women, trans women, silenced and trafficked women. After forty years out I am also aware that the voices of lesbian women are not in the #MeToo stories, as if men somehow gave us a pass, realised that we were gay and bi and queer when we were little girls, teenagers (perhaps before we did ourselves) and left us out of their predatory, possessive, prowling behaviour. But that's not what happened. All the lesbian and bi women I know have their own #MeToo stories. As usual, the spotlight has not shone on the gay women; as usual, it must be enough to ask that women be listened to at all, let alone acknowledge the voices of those of us truly beyond the pale, who will never be the helpmeet of man.

The domestic violence of my childhood meant that outside our home was often safer than inside. I am fifty-five, I have written publicly, often personally, for decades. This is the first time, as far as I can remember, that I have used the term 'domestic violence' so plainly in relation to my childhood. Cracked open emotionally as well as physically by a second cancer four years ago, I am no longer willing to leave the correct term whispered or unused.

At twelve, perhaps thirteen, this shifted, outside was no longer safe. Nowhere was safe.

He was the friend of my parents who kissed me whenever he could get away with it, few of the adults sober, he got away with it far too often. His bushy moustache probing my lips, warm hands turning a cuddle into far too much. No one to tell because what would be the point? He was a good man – such a good man that even now I am worried that writing about distinguishing marks like his facial hair might define him too much, identify him. Like countless other women, I am willing to out myself, but not the perpetrator. We are trained into silence, trained to protect men from their poor, hapless, helpless selves.

They were the boys at school who thought it was fine to decide which of us girls was the most sexually experienced. Thought it was fine to discuss this among themselves and then to let me know they had decided the girl most likely was me. Apparently I looked like I knew about sex.

What I knew back then was that I probably fancied girls more than boys, women more than men, but I had no words, no understanding, no role models. The men who leered, chased, fondled, grabbed were being true to their instincts, whereas my instinct was forbidden, disgusting, perverse.

He was the man, twenty-four to my seventeen, who drove me deep into the bush, an off-road track on an afternoon drive, and was both astonished and angry that I didn't want to fuck. Why else had I agreed to go for a drive with him? What was I doing in his car? It was a first date. Later, disappointed when I refused to answer that man's phone calls, my father was confused, annoyed, assuring me I couldn't meet a nicer lad from a nicer family.

He was the neighbour who thought it odd I wasn't interested in the beautiful cock that proved him a man – he was seventeen, I was thirteen.

And so many more.

Later in life, the same lunges, clumsy speeches, reaching hands and tongues multiplied by so many men, I wonder if they could all smell the queer on me, the queer in me, the burgeoning sexuality that I had no words for at the time.

As I began to come out more in my later teens, my early twenties, my declared lesbianism served as a challenge to certain straight men, a gauntlet thrown down. For a good fifteen years, from my early twenties until my mid-thirties, being an out gay woman made me catnip to a particular kind of straight man – men more common than my friends, their wives and girlfriends, might like to think. Luckily, depressingly, typically, that attraction died when cancer and chemotherapy turned me to menopausal crone at thirty-seven. If only we older women could gift our young sisters the cloak of invisibility that age enforces upon us.

In my teens however, my incipient awareness of my sexuality – nothing but deviant, no one but Sister George as a role model – was weird, odd, too much. I was always too much for boys. Yet at thirteen and fourteen, I was not too much for some men. And so, disturbed as I was by the tickling moustache, disgusted by the groping hands, repulsed by the beer breath, there was also a part of me – born in the sixties remember, trained to desire and accept male attention remember – that welcomed the attention. A gay girl both hating and grateful for the male gaze that made her less odd.

Until the excess of it all made me ill. Bulimic, self-harming. Enough.

Slowly a carapace grew, not yet armour but shell, attached to the skin and flesh beneath. Harder too, to prise off later when it became cumbersome, solid, brutally heavy.

Kafka's *The Metamorphosis* has a man change overnight; life has girls become women who change daily, hourly, mercury rising or falling depending on our sense of safety in any given moment. Until, eventually, heat or ice, love or loss, breaks us. The carapace cracks in our tired places, stress-tested one or ten or a thousand times too often, from our jogged elbows pushed in to make room for his big, strong arms, to our knees exhausted from years of ceding space to manspreaders, our cheeks kissed translucent with unwarranted attentions too close to lips, these mouths closed once too often, shoulder pads buckled under decades of proprietary arms, and our fondled breasts and our grabbed cunts.

Fuck off with your 'pussy-grab', my cunt is not kitten-cute.

Piece by piece the armour falls, taking strips of skin with it, wrenching gobbets of flesh, drawing blood.

We stand – I stand – revealed.

Washed out, worn, deeply scarred and very tired.

A lubrication of tears, a flicker of rage, some flexing of muscles.

The yawning gasp, gaping silent mouths, and then – slowly, trickling in, whispered one to one, thousands to thousands, seeping, rising, pouring, flowing – the flood.

A #MeToo to drown out the excuses, the reasons, the explanations.

A #MeToo that says the reasons and excuses and explanations are not the point.

This must not be a story about the perpetrators.

This must be a story about all of us, by each of us, with every voice heard.

And each one saying –

This is true. This is mine.

I'm telling my story. Me. ■

Stella Duffy (right) with Veronica, one of her six siblings, Woolwich, *c.*1967
With her mother, Leysdown, *c.*1965
And with family (front) at her First Communion, Tokoroa, New Zealand, 1970
Courtesy of the author

CROSS-DRESSERS

Sébastien Lifshitz

Introduction by Andrew McMillan

'It was the hubris of each generation to think anew, to
think that their time was special, that all things would
come to an end with them.' – Hugh Howey

T his is not a new thought, it has been articulated by other writers
in different contexts, but I admire the crispness of Howey's
assertion. And it's not just in terms of the apocalypse that we tend to
think of our own generation as pioneers.

Reading through the hyperbolic, scaremongering, inaccurate and
damaging discourse about trans people in the UK today, one might
imagine that this is a new phenomenon. These pictures, collected and
curated by French screenwriter and director Sébastien Lifshitz, tell us
that, of course, this is not true.

The fact that we've been taught to think that gender fluidity is a
new feature of our age (as opposed to just a newly visible feature)
means that Lifshitz's images can feel anachronistic, lending them
a slightly sinister or even uncanny feeling.

L ooking through these photographs, pulled out from flea markets and junk shops and the cosmic garage clearance of eBay, is like observing a scientist on the brink of a new discovery for which there isn't yet a language.

No, that's not quite right; rather the images are *haunting*, in the sense that the subjects are inhabiting a space we thought had not yet been invented.

Perhaps by *haunting* I mean that these images appear to give a glimpse of a ghost-self, a photographic negative of the heart; the parts of the self usually in shadow, brought out into the light. The observer is caught in the gaze of the poser, each seemingly on the edge of some brilliant discovery of self, but without, as yet, an adequate language to stretch beyond the binary.

O ne thing which strikes me, particularly in the images of women dressing in the traditionally masculine code of suit and bowler hat, is how fashionable they look. Fashion has cycled through such looks over the past few decades, how 'men's tailoring' or 'boyfriend jeans' are standard lexicon in women's fashion, whereas the equivalent for men, of skirts or dresses, is still kept mostly in the avant-garde.

There's something of wealth going on here as well. It's not just that these are people who could afford to have photographs taken, but their dress, too, is of a particular class. None of them are particularly exaggerating the binary gender in which they have chosen to present. This isn't drag – which seeks to be hypervisible – this is, as the title suggests, cross-dressing, which comes to us through German from the Latin of across/beyond and to dress/to clothe. The idea of moving beyond one's restrictive clothing, to move across a binary idea of dressing, across an invisible social border, as disguise, as dress-up, as a way of transitioning into the life one always felt one should have.

Some of these subjects might identify as transgender, non-binary or gender-fluid. Some of them might simply be trying something out, reaching out towards their ghost-self, and seeing if their hands pass through, or touch something solid.

These photos have come to us as postcards from the recent past to warn us of hubris: the present is not unique or special. We should not seek to comfort our ignorance by ignoring history.

I think of my favourite underwear in my early twenties being 'women's boxer shorts' because they felt tighter and more snug than the baggy male equivalents. I think of my boyfriend layering women's blouses over male jeans or a skirt or a pair of trousers, and still being a man.

I think of oppressive dress codes in schools.

I think of fashion trends which give momentary permission for clothes to cross the binary.

I think of all my brave and fierce trans friends, on their own distinct journeys into the self they always felt they were.

I think of an old photograph, of subjects having to stand still and feel stuck for what seems like an age, until slowly something beautiful begins to emerge. ∎

United States, *c.*1910

France, *c.*1920

United States, *c.*1930

United States, *c.*1920

France, *c.*1920

A woman in a doctor's uniform, France, 1902
From *Les femmes de l'avenir* (*Women of the future*), a series of satirical postcards.

A woman in a soldier's uniform, France, 1902

A young boy wearing a dress (left) and a young girl, United States, *c.*1880

United States, *c.*1880

Three women in men's suits, a man and a young boy on the Fourth of July, United States, 1912

Mock wedding, United States, *c.*1910
Mock weddings were a phenomenon that began at American colleges for women in the nineteenth century. They were banned amid concerns that they would promote feminism and celebrate homosexuality.

Mock wedding, United States, *c.*1920

Arizona, United States, 1920

n women in suits and one in a dress, United States, *c.*1920

Germany, *c.*1950

NORMAL PEOPLE

Sally Rooney

After the first time they had sex, Marianne stayed the night in his house. He had never been with a girl who was a virgin before. In total he had only had sex a small number of times, and always with girls who went on to tell the whole school about it afterwards. He'd had to hear his actions repeated back to him later in the locker room: his errors, and, so much worse, his excruciating attempts at tenderness, performed in gigantic pantomime. With Marianne it was different, because everything was between them only, even awkward or difficult things. He could do or say anything he wanted with her and no one would ever find out. It gave him a vertiginous, light-headed feeling to think about it. When he touched her that night she was so wet, and she rolled her eyes back into her head and said: God, yes. And she was allowed to say it, no one would know. He was afraid he would come then just from touching her like that.

In the hallway the next morning he kissed her goodbye and her mouth tasted alkaline, like toothpaste. Thanks, she said. Then she left, before he understood what he was being thanked for. He put the bedsheets in the washing machine and took fresh linen from the hot press. He was thinking about what a secretive, independent-minded person Marianne was, that she could come over to his house and let him have sex with her, and she felt no need to tell anyone about it.

She just let things happen, like nothing meant anything to her.

Lorraine got home that afternoon. Before she'd even put her keys on the table she said: Is that the washing machine? Connell nodded. She crouched down and looked through the round glass window into the drum, where his sheets were tossing around in the froth.

I'm not going to ask, she said.

What?

She started to fill the kettle, while he leaned against the countertop.

Why your bedclothes are in the wash, she said. I'm not asking.

He rolled his eyes just for something to do with his face.

You think the worst of everything, he said.

She laughed, fixing the kettle into its cradle and hitting the switch. Excuse me, she said. I must be the most permissive mother of anyone in your school. As long as you're using protection, you can do what you want.

He said nothing. The kettle started to warm up and she took a clean mug down from the press.

Well? she said. Is that a yes?

Yes what? Obviously I didn't have unprotected sex with anyone while you were gone. Jesus.

So go on, what's her name?

He left the room then but he could hear his mother laughing as he went up the stairs. His life was always giving her amusement.

In school on Monday he had to avoid looking at Marianne or interacting with her in any way. He carried the secret around like something large and hot, like an overfull tray of hot drinks that he had to carry everywhere and never spill. She just acted the same as always, like it never happened, reading her book at the lockers as usual, getting into pointless arguments. At lunchtime on Tuesday, Rob started asking questions about Connell's mother working in Marianne's house, and Connell just ate his lunch and tried not to make any facial expressions.

Would you ever go in there yourself? Rob said. Into the mansion.

Connell jogged his bag of chips in his hand and then peered into it. I've been in there a few times, yeah, he said.

What's it like inside?

He shrugged. I don't know, he said. Big, obviously. What's she like in her natural habitat? Rob said.

I don't know.

I'd say she thinks of you as her butler, does she?

Connell wiped his mouth with the back of his hand. It felt greasy. His chips were too salty and he had a headache.

I doubt it, Connell said.

But your mam is her housemaid, isn't she?

Well, she's just a cleaner. She's only there like twice a week, I don't think they interact much.

Does Marianne not have a little bell she would ring to get her attention, no? Rob said.

Connell said nothing. He didn't understand the situation with Marianne at that point. After he talked to Rob he told himself it was over, he'd just had sex with her once to see what it was like, and he wouldn't see her again. Even as he was saying all this to himself, however, he could hear another part of his brain, in a different voice, saying: Yes you will. It was a part of his consciousness he had never really known before, this inexplicable drive to act on perverse and secret desires. He found himself fantasising about her in class that afternoon, at the back of Maths, or when they were supposed to be playing rounders. He would think of her small wet mouth and suddenly run out of breath, and have to struggle to fill his lungs.

That afternoon he went to her house after school. All the way over in the car he kept the radio on very loud so he didn't have to think about what he was doing. When they went upstairs he didn't say anything, he let her talk. That's so good, she kept saying. That feels so good. Her body was all soft and white like flour dough. He seemed to fit perfectly inside her. Physically it just felt right, and he understood why people did insane things for sexual reasons then. In fact he understood a lot of things about the adult world that had previously seemed mysterious. But why Marianne? It wasn't like she was so attractive. Some people thought she was the ugliest girl in school. What kind of person would want to do this with her? And yet he was there, whatever kind of person he was, doing it. She asked him if it felt good and he pretended he didn't hear her. She was on her hands and knees so he couldn't see her facial expression or read into it what she was thinking. After a few seconds she said in a much smaller voice: Am I doing something wrong? He closed his eyes.

No, he said. I like it.

Her breath sounded ragged then. He pulled her hips back against his body and then released her slightly. She made a noise like she was choking. He did it again and she told him she was going to come. That's good, he said. He said this like nothing could be more ordinary to him. His decision to drive to Marianne's house that afternoon suddenly seemed very correct and intelligent, maybe the only intelligent thing he had ever done in his life. After they were finished he asked her what he should do with the condom. Without lifting her face off the pillow she said: You can just leave it on the floor. Her face was pink and damp. He did what she said and then lay on his back looking up at the light fixtures. I like you so much, Marianne said. Connell felt a pleasurable sorrow come over him, which brought him close to tears. Moments of emotional pain arrived like this, meaningless or at least indecipherable. Marianne lived a drastically free life, he could see that. He was trapped by various considerations. He cared what people thought of him. He even cared what Marianne thought, that was obvious now.

Multiple times he has tried writing his thoughts about Marianne down on paper in an effort to make sense of them. He's moved by a desire to describe in words exactly how she looks and speaks. Her hair and clothing. The copy of *Swann's Way* she reads at lunchtime in the school cafeteria, with a dark French painting on the cover and a mint-coloured spine. Her long fingers turning the pages. She's not leading the same kind of life as other people. She acts so worldly at times, making him feel ignorant, but then she can be so naive. He wants to understand how her mind works. If he silently decides not to say something when they're talking, Marianne will ask 'what?' within one or two seconds. This 'what?' question seems to him to contain so much: not just the forensic attentiveness to his silences that allows her to ask in the first place, but a desire for total communication, a sense that anything unsaid is an unwelcome interruption between them. He writes these things down, long run-on sentences with too many dependent clauses, sometimes connected with breathless semicolons, as if he wants to recreate a precise copy of Marianne in print, as if he can preserve her completely for future review. Then he turns a new page in the notebook so he doesn't have to look at what he's done.

What are you thinking about? says Marianne now.

She's tucking her hair behind her ear. College, he says.

You should apply for English in Trinity.

He stares at the web page again. Lately he's consumed by a sense that he is in fact two separate people, and soon he will have to choose which person to be on a full-time basis, and leave the other person behind. He has a life in Carricklea, he has friends. If he went to college in Galway he could stay with the same social group, really, and live the life he has always planned on, getting a good degree, having a nice girlfriend. People would say he had done well for himself. On the other hand, he could go to Trinity like Marianne. Life would be different then. He would start going to dinner parties and having conversations about the Greek bailout. He could fuck some weird-looking girls who turn out to be bisexual. I've read *The Golden Notebook*, he could tell them. It's true, he has read it. After that he would never come back to Carricklea, he would go somewhere else, London, or Barcelona. People would not necessarily think he had done well; some people might think he had gone very bad, while others would forget about him entirely. What would Lorraine think? She would want him to be happy, and not care what others said. But the old Connell, the one all his friends know: that person would be dead in a way, or worse, buried alive, and screaming under the earth.

Then we'd both be in Dublin, he says. I bet you'd pretend you didn't know me if we bumped into each other.

Marianne says nothing at first. The longer she stays silent the more nervous he feels, like maybe she really would pretend not to know him, and the idea of being beneath her notice gives him a panicked feeling, not only about Marianne personally but about his future, about what's possible for him.

Then she says: I would never pretend not to know you, Connell.

The silence becomes very intense after that. For a few seconds he lies still. Of course, he pretends not to know Marianne in school, but he didn't mean to bring that up. That's just the way it has to be. If people found out what he has been doing with Marianne, in secret, while ignoring her every day in school, his life would be over. He would walk down the hallway and people's eyes would follow him, like he was a serial killer, or worse. His friends don't think of him as a deviant person, a person who could say to Marianne Sheridan, in broad daylight, completely sober: Is it okay if I come in your mouth? With his friends he acts normal. He and Marianne have their own private life in his room where no one can bother them, so there's no reason to mix up the separate worlds. Still, he can tell he has lost his footing in their discussion and left an opening for this subject to arise, though he didn't want it to, and now he has to say something.

Would you not? he says.

No.

Alright, I'll put down English in Trinity, then.

Really? she says.

Yeah. I don't care that much about getting a job anyway.

She gives him a little smile, like she feels she has won the argument. He likes to give her that feeling. For a moment it seems possible to keep both worlds, both versions of his life, and to move in between them just like moving through a door. He can have the respect of someone like Marianne and also be well liked in school, he can form secret opinions and preferences, no conflict has to arise, he never has to choose one thing over another. With only a little subterfuge he can live two entirely separate existences, never confronting the ultimate question of what to do with himself or what kind of person he is.

This thought is so consoling that for a few seconds he avoids meeting Marianne's eye, wanting to sustain the belief for just a little longer. He knows that when he looks at her, he won't be able to believe it any more.

Six Weeks Later (April 2011)

They have her name on a list. She shows the bouncer her ID. When she gets inside, the interior is low-lit, cavernous, vaguely purple, with long bars on either side and steps down to a dance floor. It smells of stale alcohol and the flat tinny ring of dry ice. Some of the other girls from the fundraising committee are sitting around a table already, looking at lists. Hi, Marianne says. They turn around and look at her.

Hello, says Lisa. Don't you scrub up well?

You look gorgeous, says Karen.

Rachel Moran says nothing. Everyone knows that Rachel is the most popular girl in school, but no one is allowed to say this. Instead everyone has to pretend not to notice that their social lives are arranged hierarchically, with certain people at the top, some jostling at mid-level, and others lower down. Marianne sometimes sees herself at the very bottom of the ladder, but at other times she pictures herself off the ladder completely, not affected by its mechanics, since she does not actually desire popularity or do anything to make it belong to her. From her vantage point it is not obvious what rewards the ladder provides, even to those who really are at the top. She rubs her upper arm and says: Thanks. Would anyone like a drink? I'm going to the bar anyway.

I thought you didn't drink alcohol, says Rachel.

I'll have a bottle of West Coast Cooler, Karen says. If you're sure.

Wine is the only alcoholic beverage Marianne has ever tried, but when she goes to the bar she decides to order a gin and tonic. The barman looks frankly at her breasts while she's talking. Marianne had no idea men really did such things outside of films and TV, and the experience gives her a little thrill of femininity. She's wearing a filmy black dress that clings to her body. The place is still almost empty now, though the event has technically started. Back at the table Karen thanks her extravagantly for the drink. I'll get you back, she says. Don't worry about it, says Marianne, waving her hand.

Eventually people start arriving. The music comes on, a pounding Destiny's Child remix, and Rachel gives Marianne the book of raffle tickets and explains the pricing system. Marianne was voted onto the Debs fundraising committee presumably as some kind of joke, but she has to help organise the events anyway. Ticket book in hand, she continues to hover beside the other girls. She's used to observing these people from a distance, almost scientifically, but tonight, having to make conversation and smile politely, she's no longer an observer but an intruder, and an awkward one. She sells some tickets, dispensing change from the pouch in her purse, she buys more drinks, she glances at the door and looks away in disappointment.

The lads are fairly late, says Lisa.

Of all the possible lads, Marianne knows who is specified: Rob, with whom Lisa has an on-again off-again relationship, and his friends Eric, Jack Hynes and Connell Waldron. Their lateness has not escaped Marianne's notice.

If they don't show up I will actually murder Connell, says Rachel. He told me yesterday they were definitely coming.

Marianne says nothing. Rachel often talks about Connell this way, alluding to private conversations that have happened between them, as if they are special confidants. Connell ignores this behaviour, but he also ignores the hints Marianne drops about it when they're alone together.

They're probably still pre-drinking in Rob's, says Lisa.

They'll be absolutely binned by the time they get here, says Karen.

Marianne takes her phone from her bag and writes Connell a text message: Lively discussion here on the subject of your absence. Are you planning to come at all? Within thirty seconds he replies: yeah jack just got sick everywhere so we had to put him in a taxi etc.

on our way soon though. how are you getting on socialising with people. Marianne writes back: I'm the new popular girl in school now. Everyone's carrying me around the dance floor chanting my name. She puts her phone back in her bag. Nothing would feel more exhilarating to her at this moment than to say: They'll be on their way shortly. How much terrifying and bewildering status would accrue to her in this one moment, how destabilising it would be, how destructive.

Although Carricklea is the only place Marianne has ever lived, it's not a town she knows particularly well. She doesn't go drinking in the pubs on Main Street, and before tonight she had never been to the town's only nightclub. She has never visited the Knocklyon housing estate. She doesn't know the name of the river that runs brown and bedraggled past the Centra and behind the church car park, snagging thin plastic bags in its current, or where the river goes next. Who would tell her? The only time she leaves the house is to go to school, and the enforced Mass trip on Sundays, and to Connell's house when no one is home. She knows how long it takes to get to Sligo town – twenty minutes – but the locations of other nearby towns, and their sizes in relation to Carricklea, are a mystery to her. Coolaney, Skreen, Ballysadare, she's pretty sure these are all in the vicinity of Carricklea, and the names ring bells for her in a vague way, but she doesn't know where they are. She's never been inside the sports centre. She's never gone drinking in the abandoned hat factory, though she has been driven past it in the car.

Likewise, it's impossible for her to know which families in town are considered good families and which aren't. It's the kind of thing she would like to know, just to be able to reject it the more completely. She's from a good family and Connell is from a bad one, that much she does know. The Waldrons are notorious in Carricklea. One of Lorraine's brothers was in prison once, Marianne doesn't know for what, and another one got into a motorcycle crash off the roundabout a few years ago and almost died. And of course, Lorraine got pregnant at seventeen and left school to have the baby. Nonetheless Connell is considered quite a catch these days. He's studious, he plays centre forward in football, he's good-looking, he doesn't get into fights. Everybody likes him. He's quiet. Even Marianne's mother will say approvingly: That boy is nothing like a Waldron. Marianne's mother is a solicitor. Her father was a solicitor too.

Last week, Connell mentioned something called 'the ghost'.

Marianne had never heard of it before, she had to ask him what it was. His eyebrows shot up. The ghost, he said. The ghost estate, Mountain View. It's like, right behind the school. Marianne had been vaguely aware of some construction on the land behind the school, but she didn't know there was a housing estate there now, or that no one lived in it. People go drinking there, Connell added. Oh, said Marianne. She asked what it was like. He said he wished he could show her, but there were always people around. He often makes blithe remarks about things he 'wishes'. I wish you didn't have to go, he says when she's leaving, or: I wish you could stay the night. If he really wished for any of those things, Marianne knows, then they would happen. Connell always gets what he wants, and then feels sorry for himself when what he wants doesn't make him happy.

Anyway, he did end up taking her to see the ghost estate. They drove there in his car one afternoon and he went out first to make sure no one was around before she followed him. The houses were huge, with bare concrete facades and overgrown front lawns. Some of the empty window holes were covered over in plastic sheeting, which whipped around loudly in the wind. It was raining and she had left her jacket in the car. She crossed her arms, squinting up at the wet slate roofs.

Do you want to look inside? Connell said.

The front door of number 23 was unlocked. It was quieter in the house, and darker. The place was filthy. With the toe of her shoe Marianne prodded at an empty cider bottle. There were cigarette butts all over the floor and someone had dragged a mattress into the otherwise bare living room. The mattress was stained badly with damp and what looked like blood.

P retty sordid, Marianne said aloud. Connell was quiet, just looking around.

Do you hang out here much? she said.

He gave a kind of shrug. Not much, he said. Used to a bit, not much any more.

Please tell me you've never had sex on that mattress.

He smiled absently. No, he said. Is that what you think I get up to at the weekend, is it?

Kind of.

He didn't say anything then, which made her feel even worse. He kicked a crushed can of Dutch Gold aimlessly and sent it skidding towards the French doors.

This is probably three times the size of my house, he said.

Would you say?

She felt foolish for not realising what he had been thinking about. Probably, she said. I haven't seen upstairs, obviously.

Four bedrooms.

Jesus.

Just lying empty, no one living in it, he said. Why don't they give them away if they can't sell them? I'm not being thick with you, I'm genuinely asking.

She shrugged. She didn't actually understand why. It's something to do with capitalism, she said.

Yeah. Everything is, that's the problem, isn't it?

She nodded. He looked over at her, as if coming out of a dream. Are you cold? he said. You look like you're freezing.

She smiled, rubbed at her nose. He unzipped his black Puffa jacket and put it over her shoulders. They were standing very close. She would have lain on the ground and let him walk over her body if he wanted, he knew that.

When I go out at the weekend or whatever, he said, I don't go after other girls or anything.

Marianne smiled and said: No, I guess they come after you.

He grinned, he looked down at his shoes. You have a very funny idea of me, he said.

She closed her fingers around his school tie. It was the first time in her life she could say shocking things and use bad language, so she did it a lot. If I wanted you to fuck me here, she said, would you do it?

His expression didn't change but his hands moved around under her jumper to show he was listening. After a few seconds he said: Yeah. If you wanted to, yeah. You're always making me do such weird things.

What does that mean? she said. I can't make you do anything.

Yeah, you can. Do you think there's any other person I would do this type of thing with? Seriously, do you think anyone else could make me sneak around after school and all this?

What do you want me to do? Leave you alone?

He looked at her, seemingly taken aback by this turn in the discussion. Shaking his head, he said: If you did that . . .

She looked at him but he didn't say anything else. If I did that, what? she said.

I don't know. You mean, if you just didn't want to see each other any more? I would feel surprised honestly, because you seem like you enjoy it.

And what if I met someone else who liked me more?

He laughed. She turned away crossly, pulling out of his grasp, wrapping her arms around her chest. He said hey, but she didn't turn around. She was facing the disgusting mattress with the rust-coloured stains all over it. Gently he came up behind her and lifted her hair to kiss the back of her neck.

Sorry for laughing, he said. You're making me insecure, talking about not wanting to hang out with me any more. I thought you liked me.

She shut her eyes. I do like you, she said.

Well, if you met someone else you liked more, I'd be pissed off, okay? Since you ask about it. I wouldn't be happy. Alright?

Your friend Eric called me flat-chested today in front of everyone.

Connell paused. She felt his breathing. I didn't hear that, he said.

You were in the bathroom or somewhere. He said I looked like an ironing board.

Fuck's sake, he's such a prick. Is that why you're in a bad mood? She shrugged. Connell put his arms around her belly.

He's only trying to get on your nerves, he said. If he thought he had the slightest chance with you, he would be talking very differently. He just thinks you look down on him.

She shrugged again, chewing on her lower lip.

You have nothing to worry about with your appearance, Connell said.

Hm.

I don't just like you for your brains, trust me.

She laughed, feeling silly.

He rubbed her ear with his nose and added: I would miss you if you didn't want to see me any more.

Would you miss sleeping with me? she said.

He touched his hand against her hip bone, rocking her back against his body, and said quietly: Yeah, a lot.

Can we go back to your house now?

He nodded. For a few seconds they just stood there in stillness, his arms around her, his breath on her ear. Most people go through their whole lives, Marianne thought, without ever really feeling that close with anyone.

Finally, after her third gin and tonic, the door bangs open and the boys arrive. The committee girls get up and start teasing them, scolding them for being late, things like that. Marianne hangs back, searching for Connell's eye contact, which he doesn't return. He's dressed in a white button-down shirt, the same Adidas sneakers he wears everywhere. The other boys are wearing shirts too, but more formal-looking, shinier, and worn with leather dress shoes. There's a heavy, stirring smell of aftershave in the air. Eric catches Marianne's eye and suddenly lets go of Karen, a move obvious enough that everyone else looks around too.

Look at you, Marianne, says Eric.

She can't tell immediately whether he's being sincere or mocking. All the boys are looking at her now except Connell.

I'm serious, Eric says. Great dress, very sexy.

Rachel starts laughing, leans in to say something in Connell's ear. He turns his face away slightly and doesn't laugh along. Marianne feels a certain pressure in her head that she wants to relieve by screaming or crying.

Let's go and have a dance, says Karen.

I've never seen Marianne dancing, Rachel says.

Well, you can see her now, says Karen.

Karen takes Marianne's hand and pulls her towards the dance floor. There's a Kanye West song playing, the one with the Curtis Mayfield sample. Marianne is still holding the raffle book in one hand, and she feels the other hand damp inside Karen's. The dance floor is crowded and sends shudders of bass up through her shoes into her legs. Karen props an arm on Marianne's shoulder, drunkenly, and says in her ear: Don't mind Rachel, she's in foul humour. Marianne nods her head, moving her body in time with the music. Feeling drunk now, she turns to search the room, wanting to know where Connell is. Right away she sees him, standing at the top of the steps. He's watching her. The music is so loud it throbs inside her body. Around him the others are talking and laughing. He's just looking at her and saying nothing. Under his gaze her movements feel magnified, scandalous, and the weight of Karen's arm on her shoulder is sensual and hot. She rocks her hips forward and runs a hand loosely through her hair.

In her ear Karen says: He's been watching you the whole time.

Marianne looks at him and then back at Karen, saying nothing, trying not to let her face say anything.

Now you see why Rachel's in a bad mood with you, says Karen.

She can smell the wine spritzer on Karen's breath when she speaks, she can see her fillings. She likes her so much at that moment. They dance a little more and then go back upstairs together, hand in hand, out of breath now, grinning about nothing. Eric and Rob are pretending to have an argument. Connell moves towards Marianne almost imperceptibly, and their arms touch. She wants to pick up his hand and suck on his fingertips one after another.

Rachel turns to her then and says: You might try actually selling some raffle tickets at some point?

Marianne smiles, and the smile that comes out is smug, almost derisive, and she says: Okay.

I think these lads might want to buy some, says Eric.

He nods over at the door, where some older guys have arrived. They're not supposed to be here, the nightclub said it would be ticket-holders only. Marianne doesn't know who they are, someone's brothers or cousins maybe, or just men in their twenties who like to hang around school fundraisers. They see Eric waving and come over. Marianne looks in her purse for the cash pouch in case they do want to buy raffle tickets.

How are things, Eric? says one of the men. Who's your friend here?

That's Marianne Sheridan, Eric says. You'd know her brother, I'd say. Alan, he would've been in Mick's year.

The man just nods, looking Marianne up and down. She feels indifferent to his attention. The music is too loud to hear what Rob is saying in Eric's ear, but Marianne feels it has to do with her.

Let me get you a drink, the man says. What are you having?

No, thanks, says Marianne.

The man slips an arm around her shoulders then. He's very tall, she notices. Taller than Connell. His fingers rub her bare arm. She tries to shrug him off but he doesn't let go. One of his friends starts laughing, and Eric laughs along.

Nice dress, the man says.

Can you let go of me? she says.

Very low-cut there, isn't it?

In one motion he moves his hand down from her shoulder and squeezes the flesh of her right breast, in front of everyone. Instantly she jerks away from him, pulling her dress up to her collarbone, feeling her face fill with blood. Her eyes are stinging and she feels a pain where he grabbed her. Behind her the others are laughing. She can hear them. Rachel is laughing, a high fluting noise in Marianne's ears.

Without turning around, Marianne walks out the door, lets it slam behind her. She's in the hallway now with the cloakroom and can't remember whether the exit is right or left. She's shaking all over her body. The cloakroom attendant asks if she's alright. Marianne doesn't know any more how drunk she is. She walks a few steps towards a door on the left and then puts her back against the wall and starts sliding down towards a seated position on the floor. Her breast is aching where that man grabbed it. He wasn't joking, he wanted to hurt her. She's on the floor now hugging her knees against her chest.

Up the hall the door comes open again and Karen comes out, with Eric and Rachel and Connell following. They see Marianne on the floor and Karen runs over to her while the other three stay standing where they are, not knowing what to do maybe, or not wanting to do anything. Karen hunches down in front of Marianne and touches her hand. Marianne's eyes are sore and she doesn't know where to look.

Are you alright? Karen says.

I'm fine, says Marianne. I'm sorry. I think I just had too much to drink.

Leave her, says Rachel.

Here, look, it was just a bit of fun, says Eric. Pat's actually a sound enough guy if you get to know him.

I think it was funny, says Rachel.

At this Karen snaps around and looks at them. Why are you even out here if you think it was so funny? she says. Why don't you go and pal around with your best friend Pat? If you think it's so funny to molest young girls?

How is Marianne *young*? says Eric.

We were all laughing at the time, says Rachel.

That's not true, says Connell.

Everyone looks around at him then. Marianne looks at him. Their eyes meet.

Are you okay, are you? he says.

Oh, do you want to kiss her better? says Rachel.

His face is flushed now, and he touches a hand to his brow. Everyone is still watching him. The wall feels cold against Marianne's back.

Rachel, he says, would you ever fuck off?

Karen and Eric exchange a look then, eyes wide, Marianne can see them. Connell never speaks or acts like this in school. In all these years she has never seen him behave at all aggressively, even when taunted. Rachel just tosses her head and walks back inside the club. The door falls shut heavily on its hinges. Connell continues rubbing his brow for a second. Karen mouths something at Eric, Marianne doesn't know what it is. Then Connell looks at Marianne and says: Do you want to go home? I'm driving, I can drop you. She nods her head. Karen helps her up from the floor. Connell puts his hands in his pockets as if to prevent himself touching her by accident. Sorry for making a fuss, Marianne says to Karen. I feel stupid. I'm not used to drinking.

It's not your fault, says Karen.

Thank you for being so nice, Marianne says.

They squeeze hands once more. Marianne follows Connell towards the exit then and around the side of the hotel, to where his car is parked. It's dark and cool out here, with the sound of music from the nightclub pulsing faintly behind them. She gets in the passenger seat and puts her seat belt on. He closes the driver's door and puts his keys in the ignition.

Sorry for making a fuss, she says again.

You didn't, says Connell. I'm sorry the others were being so stupid about it. They just think Pat is great because he has these parties in his house sometimes. Apparently if you have house parties it's okay to mess with people, I don't know.

It really hurt. What he did.

Connell says nothing then. He just kneads the steering wheel with his hands. He looks down into his lap, and exhales quickly, almost like a cough. Sorry, he says. Then he starts the car. They drive for a few minutes in silence, Marianne cooling her forehead against the window.

Do you want to come back to my house for a bit? he says.

Is Lorraine not there?

He shrugs. He taps his fingers on the wheel. She's probably in bed already, he says. I mean we could just hang out for a bit before I drop you home. It's okay if you don't want to.

What if she's still up?

Honestly she's pretty relaxed about this sort of stuff anyway. Like I really don't think she would care.

Marianne stares out the window at the passing town. She knows what he's saying: that he doesn't mind if his mother finds out about them. Maybe she already knows.

Lorraine seems like a really good parent, Marianne remarks.

Yeah. I think so.

She must be proud of you. You're the only boy in school who's actually turned out well as an adult.

Connell glances over at her. How have I turned out well? he says.

What do you mean? Everyone likes you. And unlike most people you're actually a nice person.

He makes a facial expression she can't interpret, kind of raising his eyebrows, or frowning. When they get back to his house the windows are all dark and Lorraine is in bed. In Connell's room he and Marianne lie down together whispering. He tells her that she's beautiful. She has never heard that before, though she has sometimes privately suspected it of herself, but it feels different to hear it from another person. She touches his hand to her breast where it hurts, and he kisses her. Her face is wet, she's been crying. He kisses her neck. Are you okay? he says. When she nods, he smooths her hair back and says: It's alright to be upset, you know. She lies with her face against his chest. She feels like a soft piece of cloth that is wrung out and dripping.

You would never hit a girl, would you? she says.

God, no. Of course not. Why would you ask that?

I don't know.

Do you think I'm the kind of person who would go around hitting girls? he says.

She presses her face very hard against his chest. My dad used to hit my mum, she says. For a few seconds, which seems like an unbelievably long time, Connell says nothing. Then he says: Jesus. I'm sorry. I didn't know that.

It's okay, she says.

Did he ever hit you?

Sometimes.

Connell is silent again. He leans down and kisses her on the forehead. I would never hurt you, okay? he says. Never. She nods and says nothing. You make me really happy, he says. His hand moves over her hair and he adds: I love you. I'm not just saying that, I really do. Her eyes fill up with tears again and she closes them. Even in memory she will find this moment unbearably intense, and she's aware of this now, while it's happening. She has never believed herself fit to be loved by any person. But now she has a new life, of which this is the first moment, and even after many years have passed she will still think: Yes, that was it, the beginning of my life. ■

© RICHARD PLUMRIDGE
_Narrative, 2011

COMME

Paul Dalla Rosa

The Melbourne store was in an alleyway. There was nothing in the alleyway, only red bricks and the store. We had no signage though people persistently stood in front of the entrance and took photos of themselves. Sometimes they would do this inside. In these situations, my staff were often unsure how to act. I told them to do what we always did, stand and wait for customers.

We played no music. Clothes hung from metal scaffolding. In shifts, time dilated. When customers appeared, they moved or seemed to move faster within the store than they did outside of it. I trained my staff to act indifferently towards them and pour cucumber water, at their discretion, for potential high-end clientele. These were mainly rich men and women from Beijing and Shanghai, or Asian teenagers using Amex platinum cards.

When the store was empty, it was almost always empty, I would use a hand-held steamer to steam items before rehanging them or I would track sales on a tablet. In all things I would aim, by example, to be very still, almost meditative. More than anything, I explained to new employees, the store was meant to be like a static image, a photograph in a magazine, dynamic only through shifts of light, the bold cuts of hemlines, a shirt's silhouette.

It was like this, the store vacant, me standing over the tablet, when the email came. It was brief and from our Asia-Pacific head of sales, a severe woman named Janelle who was based in Japan and whom I sometimes had video conferences with. She said that R, the founder of our label, would be coming. R would be in the country in two weeks' time on personal matters, but would, potentially, visit the store. 'You understand the gravity of this.'

I read the email three times. One after another, after another.

R was known for being reclusive. In the early eighties, she had arrived at Paris Fashion Week with a staff of four. What she did there shocked people. Models walked in black upon black distressed fabric, asymmetric cuts. Now she employed over 500 and had retrospectives at the Pompidou, the Met. A fellow Japanese woman, a fan, had once attempted to throw acid on her. Fashion bloggers at the time wrote that this was in fact an act of outsized love. I didn't have the same feelings towards her but I understood how others might.

I was uneasy with most forms of devotion. When a Silicon Valley billionaire died, a man I was seeing went out, bought flowers and left them outside one of the billionaire's stores. He described it to me. The store glowed in the night and people stood in front of it in heavy jackets and cried. In response, I said cruel things, well, really one remark that was too cutting, and then he said, We are no longer dating.

But I was a professional and I was good at my job. I managed the store to the precise specifications I had been taught or were sent through in emails from corporate. Often these emails weren't directives exactly but quotes from R, something closer to proverbs, ways of being. 'The fundamental human problem is that people are afraid of change.' 'Fashion is living, it is about every moment being alive.' I didn't often feel alive but I tailored my managerial style as best I could.

I was not afraid of change. I had worked in my position for many years, but I was in my thirties and wanted them to lead to something else. The label was young and I was approaching the point at which I wasn't. The visit would be important to something I had stopped speaking about aloud. My career.

W hen I told my boyfriend, he didn't respond directly but sent a message describing a glacier and a black sand beach. 'It's black. Really really black.'

He was in Iceland discovering himself. Those were his words. He had done so before on trips to Alaska and Taiwan, Morocco, a string of European cities. He only travelled alone. Because of the time difference, we mainly spoke at night.

I was lying in his bed. I slept in his apartment while he was away because it was more luxurious than mine – there was a doorman – and I felt anonymous in the Korean store below his building, where I bought items I would otherwise feel embarrassed to purchase together: diet tonic water, dry shampoo, a lone cucumber, Chinese slimming tea.

My boyfriend sent a photo but he sent the raw file, .CR2. I texted, 'lo-res, send lo-res', and he talked about a sauna in Reykjavik where they didn't put chlorine in the water, and so you had to shower before you entered, but you had to shower in an open space where an attendant watched to make sure you used soap.

My boyfriend's father was a Chinese artist and his mother an English translator and so he felt the pull to distinguish himself as something constant and painful. His godfather was Ai Weiwei. He brought it up whenever we met new people. I would hear, 'Ai Weiwei, Ai Weiwei'. It was like a mantra until he reached a certain age and didn't want people to make the comparison. Now, he just said he was a visual artist. There was never much art. Mainly, he stayed in his apartment taking near-nudes of himself and building his Instagram following. I wasn't related to Ai Weiwei and I didn't have rich parents. I weighed under sixty kilos, bought expensive clothes and wore them.

The photo still hadn't loaded. I messaged, 'I can't see it.' I switched my phone from Wi-Fi to mobile data.

He started describing it, the black pebbles, the grey sea.

I said, 'I can see it now,' even though I couldn't.

Then he said, 'It's sad you're not here. You had to stay for the designer.'

I texted, 'I only just found out about the designer.'

'I know. But you had to be there for it. It works out.'

I didn't feel like replying to that. An hour later my phone vibrated.

'I think you should masturbate in my bed.'

Then again.

'Send a photo.'

In the morning I showered and carefully did my skin regime. A cleanser, followed by toner, then moisturizer. Sometimes, I also used serum.

As I massaged in the moisturizer, I felt something dense and tender on the left side of my jaw. It was small and felt like a trigger point, a knotted muscle. I was familiar with them. When I slept I ground my teeth. It was a problem, causing tension headaches and, what concerned me most, chipped enamel.

I fed a pod into my boyfriend's espresso machine, relaxed my face, dressed, drank my coffee, then took the elevator down and walked to the store.

I unlocked the front door, then locked it once I was inside. I liked being there before we opened. At a specified angle, I sprayed the label's signature scent, or rather a scent based on our signature scent – not for sale but produced for this alone – twice on the bottom floor and twice again on the loft level. This was always the time I felt my thoughts were clearest.

I was conflicted as to whether to inform my staff about R. There was the possibility that if R did come they would recognize her, and, without warning, act in a way that would embarrass me. Or, even worse, almost unthinkable, they could mistake her for a customer.

As I thought this, my phone rang.

A staff member said he was sick. 'I have a breakout. It's really bad.'

'Have you tried concealer?'

'I've tried. I can't cover it. I can't cover it.'

My staff often shared their personal problems with me – break ups, embarrassing health complications, UTIs – to explain why, at little notice, they could not come to work. I allowed them to do so, or, rather, I would just stand there, my eyes lowered, nodding, and be relieved once they stopped speaking into the phone.

I said, 'Fine.' Even understaffed I could manage.

The day would be Heidi, Sara and me. Heidi was twenty-six and had strong features which made her not conventionally beautiful but something more interesting and strange. She had the kind of face that seemed to dramatically shift when looked at from different angles or in different light. This was the first thing I noticed when I interviewed her.

I knew that Heidi wanted to be the manager because she often said, 'I want to be the manager. It would suit my skill set.' I wanted to explain to her that my position was poorly paid, salaried as opposed to commissions. Some weeks my staff could earn more than I did. At the same time, I did not want to tell her this because I told no one this.

The day wasn't busy. At one point I watched Sara standing with a Japanese woman. Sara, like most of my staff, studied fashion and mistook working in retail for working in industry. This was understandable. I had once thought the same thing. She held the customer's card in one hand and one of the tablets in the other. They stood there for a long time. She shook the tablet. I walked over. She turned to me.

'It's not working. The point-of-sale is down.'

The screen lit up with a green tick.

'Oh, it's working now.'

I felt a muted sense of panic and though I didn't often take a lunch break, I took one and went to an office-supply store. I printed recent photographs of R at different events, and then a lone, recent paparazzi shot, taken on a street in Paris, of her drinking from a takeaway coffee cup. I came back and stuck them, with a torn-out page from *Vogue*, on one of the walls in the back room.

In the store's group messaging channel I explained the situation. I ended it with: 'For the next two weeks no one is calling in sick to shifts. No one is coming in late. No one is coming in hung-over. If you do, I will suspend your store discount. I will suspend everyone's store discount.'

That night, my boyfriend sent me a video of a geyser. He had taken the footage using a high frame rate and then played it back at twenty-four frames per second, slow motion. The frame showed a small circular pool. Slowly, a large bubble expanded and expanded until it was a metre, two metres into the air. It shimmered for one drawn-out moment, and then the surface tension was too great and it shot into the air. I watched it, then watched it again.

Lying in my boyfriend's bed, I couldn't say that I liked my life or that it was not full of small disappointments.

I was pretty. I was tall and slim, had delicate features, long hands and feet. My body was the kind of body that things were designed for and other gay men tended to project onto it their own resentments or desires.

When I was younger I had the problem of men falling in love with me. People would wait outside the store to speak to me or they would wait inside until I served them. Occasionally there would be large gestures of affection and control – plane tickets, hotel rooms, reservations to restaurants I could not afford but never had to pay for.

Now, I still got attention, it hadn't waned, but the value had depreciated. If a customer asked me out for a drink or to their apartment and I said I was seeing someone, they would narrow their eyes and reply that they could tell I was over thirty, probably close to thirty-five.

I often felt like I had made poor choices, that I had failed to capitalise in some generalized yet hyper-specific way. I had once learned Mandarin by slowly and persistently attending classes. I wanted to be transferred to the label's new flagship store in Beijing. The transfer never happened, and, over time, I stopped speaking the language to my boyfriend and we stopped watching Chinese films. He didn't mind.

We lived in separate apartments. We went to restaurants and exhibitions together, took photos of each other in soft light and uploaded those photos online. Often, as we lay in bed, my boyfriend would show me other men's Instagram profiles and ask if I thought they were attractive. Sometimes this made me emotional in ways I found difficult to describe.

We had threesomes with these same boys and filmed them. We were good-looking and people wanted to see themselves flattened onto a laptop's screen. Sometimes, during the act, my boyfriend would say desperate things aloud. What I mean is, he would describe his penis.

I watched a homeless man in front of the store. He wore an oversized coat and paced the alleyway, then looked through the glass and sort of leered at us or at his reflection. No one would go out to talk to him. At one stage he kept bending down and hopping back up, like he was doing squats or jumping jacks. This was over hours.

I let others take customers while I went to the loft level and pretended I was doing stocktake. Really, I browsed eBay listings on one of the tablets.

There was a married couple who ran an online store with rare stock from our label. They found pieces from old runway shows, acquired them, modelled them themselves in strange places – car parks, fast-food outlets – then put the photos online and took bids. They were based in Japan and were profiled in online magazines. The prices were what you'd imagine. Obscene.

I kept looking at a piece. It was a black padded shirt from the nineties. It was a shirt but had bulges that distended the silhouette. High fashion but not too high fashion. It felt now.

Because I spent a large amount of time convincing people to buy clothing they would never actually wear, it was easy to convince myself the same. I imagined how I would look in the shirt and I imagined R walking in and appraising my outfit, my style, my store.

Internally, in Japanese, she'd think, Yes, that is someone who knows what's going on.

This seemed worth $4,000. I made a bid.

Sara called out to me.

I came down the stairs. The store was empty and the homeless man was in front of the store window facing us. His dick was out. He was urinating onto the window and staring intently at Sara.

When he noticed me – I don't know how to say it – with his penis, he did a kind of flourish with the stream. It seemed effeminate. We stood there until he finished and shuffled away.

I called our cleaning company. They arrived hours after they said they would and used a high-pressure hose on the glass. Heidi sent me a message. 'Sara texted what happened. You should let her go home.' I resented this.

I let Sara go, and spritzed the store with room spray. Then I walked around and spritzed it again. I put a finger onto the tender spot on my jaw and pushed it.

I returned to the tablet. I tracked the store's sales figures, then I opened a new tab, looked at the shirt again, became nervous that someone might outbid me and so pre-emptively made a higher offer.

I had the package couriered express international. I had it delivered to the store, which was unprofessional but I knew someone would be able to sign for it. It arrived within three days. The package lay in the back room next to the rack that hung the Spring line we would only wheel out, after hours, for important customers.

I had a video conference with Janelle. She was in Singapore. She always took the calls in different cities with different backdrops and, in this way, seemed like a news correspondent. Every year we had at least one exchange which involved me asking her to rethink my position, while she stared off-webcam, before saying she was thinking and then stating implicitly, often explicitly, that many people wanted my role.

We spoke about numbers. We spoke about the numbers Janelle wanted to be seeing and I explained the numbers she was seeing. I told her the reactions we'd been having to the Spring line. Janelle nodded.

She asked about R's visit. If the store was ready for it. I said, 'Immaculate.'

She said, 'Heidi said you had a photo wall up.'

I said, 'How are you talking to Heidi?'

'Take the photos down. It's embarrassing. I need you to be across this. I need to know you can do it.'

'I can do it.'

'Good. That's what I want to hear.' She ended the call like in a movie. She never said goodbye.

I took the photos down, opened my jaw and closed it a few times, then stood on the shop floor. Heidi was with a customer. The woman kept pointing at a dress with a missing square of fabric in the front and Heidi was repeating that it wasn't cut out but 'deconstructed'. She repeated this monotone.

I wanted to kill myself but in a way that wouldn't actually kill me.

A man walked in. He was maybe in his fifties, but put-together, silvered hair. He was wearing a suit and sneakers, but sneakers I recognized. They were made of white Italian leather and retailed for $900. I figured he was an architect.

He stood next to the concrete plinth we kept our fragrances on. He looked at the different bottles. Heidi slowly oriented herself towards him, but she had to stay with her customer even though she knew it wouldn't be a sale.

I asked how could I help. The man had a British accent. He said he wanted something 'fresh'. I nodded.

I spoke about the scents, listing their profiles, holding each bottle before I sprayed one spray on a white stick of paper and handed it to him. He asked difficult questions. When I said, 'Notes of oxygen, pollution,' he said, 'But what does that mean?' After he held seven samples, I asked if there was a specific one he wanted to try.

He pointed to a bottle. It wasn't a signature scent but one in a series of concept lines. I sprayed his wrist and told him to let it settle, let it open on his skin.

The man smelled his wrist and nodded. He placed his arm back down by his side. We stood there quietly. Then he asked me to smell him. 'I want a second opinion.' He didn't raise his arm though, he just sort of rotated it, so his wrist was exposed, crotch level. He waited.

I bent down to smell it. I said what I would've said about any fragrance on any customer.

'It's really deepened.' I looked up at him. 'That's the one.'

I sold him two pairs of trousers, a sweater and a 100 ml bottle of perfume. It rang up at $3,784. The man left me the name of his hotel and his room number. Later, I sent a long message to my boyfriend describing the whole thing. Not because I was considering going there, but because I wanted attention. He replied instantly, 'Weird.' Then, 'I wonder if he would have paid you.' Then, a string of three cash emojis.

I laid the package on my boyfriend's bed and carefully slit the shipping tape. There was cardboard and layers of black tissue paper and then the shirt. Standing there, I already knew it was a bad decision.

I put it on and looked at my reflection in the bathroom mirror. My first thought was that I had put it on wrong – this sometimes happened with customers in the store – but I hadn't. It was bad. The padding made me think of Lisa Simpson in the episode where she dresses up as the state of Florida. It looked like I was wearing a futon. I took a photo, then googled 'Lisa Simpson Florida'. The resemblance didn't make me feel any better.

I sent an email saying I wanted to return it. The couple wrote back, immediately and politely, that they did not do refunds. They signed off together. I asked if I could do an exchange. Then I lay in the shirt and looked at my face using my phone's camera. Where the sore spot on my jaw was was a slightly raised mound. I fell asleep with my phone in my hands.

At 3 a.m., it vibrated. They had replied with a long, complicated message in Japanese I was almost certain meant no. I squinted and used Google Translate. It meant no.

I did what I felt I had to do in the situation. I went back to their site and made a separate offer on a 1996 see-through PVC vest.

The vest arrived and it was beautiful. To make myself comfortable in it, I wore it naked around my boyfriend's apartment. I planned to pair it with the Spring collection's oversized striped poplin shirt. I was into it. I wore it and thought of an elegant hand, R's hand, picking me up and placing me somewhere else.

The night she arrived in the country, I stayed back at the store. A shipment had come through but the stock hadn't synced with our system. I had to code each piece through manually and then put them back into their boxes and stack them. I wanted this done before R visited. I wanted things to be efficient.

I asked people to stay back. Everyone said no. As I closed, Heidi and Sara stood in the back room fixing their make-up. I got the sense that they were meeting other staff. Well, I overheard their conversation. A different label was having a party. It was an American label specializing in American streetwear but how American streetwear is worn in Asia. There would be photographers. I said to no one in particular, 'But it's a Wednesday night.'

The two of them giggled. I realized they were drinking. We kept very expensive champagne in a mini-fridge in the back room for certain high-profile customers.

I didn't want to make a thing of it. I used to be like this. Fun. But I didn't want them to think Heidi had authority or that I wasn't the boss. I told them to go to the party and leave the bottle. It was half full. I said I expected more from them. Then I got self-conscious and thought that was a stupid thing to say.

I stood on the empty shop floor and looked at the galvanized steel, the polished concrete, the clothes. It was dark outside and darker still in the store. I thought I should toast my future success, so I did. I drank champagne from the bottle and then went to the back room and continued counting.

At one point, I just sat in front of the back room's mirror and picked at my face. I thought, She's in the country, she's in the country. I saw myself in an airport transit lounge, business class, making conference calls, video calls. Yes, I imagined myself looking off-camera then telling someone my valued opinion. I sipped French champagne. I was drunk. Tokyo Fashion Week, Paris. I imagined being given all the things I deserved.

I was smiling. I looked at my reflection and saw the mound on my jaw was bigger. It was a pimple, cystic and rising from deep beneath the surface. Red and inflamed, it protruded from my jaw. It was obvious when I stood in profile and even worse head-on. I inhaled and exhaled.

The Korean market beneath my boyfriend's building was open late. It sold skin products that were both harsher and, in some instances, more effective than what I regularly used. They didn't fuck around with natural ingredients. Yuzu, neroli blossoms. They were chemical, all about results.

I asked the attendant for the strongest product they had. She handed me a foil packet that didn't really look any different from the others. It showed a smiling Korean woman. They all showed smiling Korean women.

'This is the strongest?'

The woman nodded. I pointed at my face. She whispered, 'Chemical peel.'

Back in my boyfriend's apartment, I cut cucumber slices and opened the foil packaging. It wasn't a cream but a black fold-out mask. I put it on. I lay down on the bed and placed one cucumber slice over one eye and then another on the other. I stayed like that for a while. My face slightly tingled. It was boring. I took the cucumber slices off, rolled onto my side and looked at my phone.

My boyfriend had uploaded a photo of himself, naked, his back to the camera, standing before a waterfall, his olive skin soft against jagged, volcanic rock. There were comments made by attractive people.

I knew he had a camera with a self-timer and a tripod, but the angle wasn't right. I wanted to ask who took the photo but I didn't. Instead I double-tapped it. I gave it a like.

Slowly, I felt a burning. At first, it was the kind you feel when you peroxide your hair. That sensation on the scalp. It intensified. I tore the mask off.

In the bathroom, I gagged. My face was slightly pink but the lump was larger and had a big yellow head. I told myself not to touch it. I touched it – it leaked.

I panicked. This was after midnight. I took the elevator to the foyer and ordered an Uber to the hospital. Drivers kept cancelling as they realized my destination. The doorman watched me. I went onto the street and hailed a taxi. The driver asked if I wanted emergency. I hesitated. There wasn't anywhere else to go.

Outside the hospital were women in tracksuit pants smoking cigarettes. There was a man in a white gown leaning against his IV stand. They were lit by the red emergency sign.

Inside, a toddler rolled around on the linoleum floor and an Indian couple watched something on a phone, but without headphones. A studio laugh track played and played. Everyone's clothes were synthetic and cheap.

I waited in line for triage. I picked up an old fashion magazine. It was sticky. I put the magazine down.

When I got to the front I spoke to a nurse through a little Perspex grille. She said, 'What's your emergency?'

I pointed at my jaw.

'Do you have a fever?'

'No.'

'Nausea?'

'No.'

'Okay.' She leaned forward to look at me. 'This is not an emergency. It's not appropriate for you to be here. You have a boil. I'm going to ask you to leave and to see your general practitioner.'

I said, 'I thought you had to see everyone.'

'That is a common misconception.' She closed the grille.

I walked eight blocks home.

I woke up late, close to ten. The store wouldn't open till eleven. I texted Heidi to come in early, spray the room spray, prep the store. I'd be there when we opened.

Then I stood in front of the bathroom mirror and squeezed. It was like a certain kind of YouTube video. It was disgusting, full of many horrifying things.

When I was done, I had to wash the mirror and wash my face. I spent a long time deciding whether or not to put toner on or apply moisturizer. The internet seemed inconclusive. I was very calm.

I texted Heidi to not open the store until I arrived. I dressed. The wound was weeping so I pressed a make-up pad on it and applied pressure.

Then Heidi replied.

'She's here.'

I was on the street and the icon of my Uber was moving towards me, then making turns I could not understand, and turns after those turns I understood even less. And then I was just running, my coat flaring behind me, and I thought, I am being dramatic, I am being dramatic, but I kept going and going and going. It took me ten minutes to get there, only ten minutes, and when I reached the store Heidi was standing in the doorway.

'She's gone.'

Heidi was in black kimono-like pants and a white satin collared shirt from the Spring collection. Close to dawn, she had had her hair bleached and toned. She was brilliant in the store's light.

I was still in my raincoat. I was sweating under it and the vest. I made the decision to take nothing off.

Heidi stepped out of the doorway and said, 'What happened to your face?'

There were two customers inside the store, two Asian women with designer bags. I narrowed my eyes but neither of them was R.

I said, 'What did she do?'

'She came inside. She was in all black. She looked at the store, picked a few things up, put them down. She nodded, then went into the alley and her driver took her away.'

I didn't know it at the time, but later that day I would send a series of messages to my boyfriend, each message longer than the last. I would describe my life. The circumstances as I saw them. That Heidi would replace me, that others would replace me, and I would be lucky to find a position in a large department store that would play Christmas carols from the start of every November to the beginning of every January. That my good credit rating would now be a bad credit rating but, like all the times before, would slowly equalize. And that for most of my life I desired things I thought were stupid to desire but desired all the same.

He would reply, deep in the night, with a sad-face emoji and then a photo of his penis with the caption 'Can't host', which I would understand he meant to send to someone else. This would not shock me.

But there I was, standing on the threshold of the store but not in the store. I asked Heidi if she spoke to R and what R had said. Heidi thought for a while. She kept her lips together, then opened them.

'Thank you. She said, "Thank you."' ■

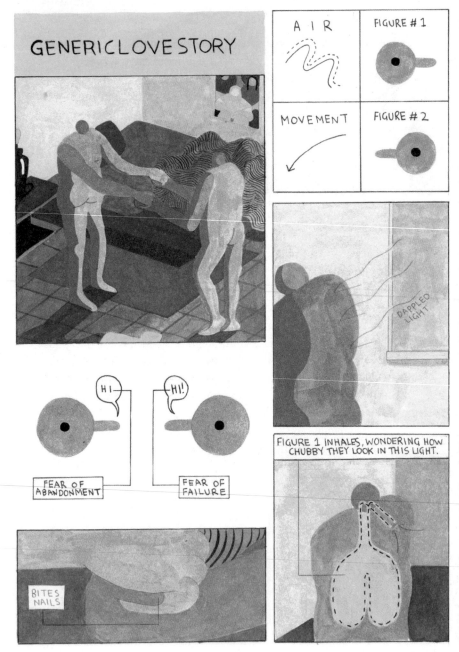

FIGURE 1 CAN'T DECIDE IF THEY FEEL LIKE FOOLING AROUND RIGHT NOW. THIS NERVOUSNESS AROUND ASSERTING BOUNDARIES IS LARGELY DUE TO UNFAIR EMOTIONAL AND SEXUAL EXPECTATIONS FORCED ONTO FIGURE 1 BY SOCIETY.

IN / OUT

FIGURE 2 BREATHES OUT AT THE SAME MOMENT AND TRIES TO APPEAR CALM. REF: FEAR OF ABANDONMENT.

← STEP

FIGURE 2 IS CURRENTLY 'ONLY A BIT GAY SOMETIMES' WHICH IS CONFUSING AND A SOURCE OF ANXIETY.

FIGURE 1 BRIEFLY SMOKED IN HIGH-SCHOOL BUT QUIT AFTER LEARNING THEIR MOTHER DIDN'T MIND.

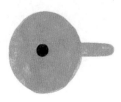

FIGURE 2'S FAVOURITE BAND IS SILVERCHAIR.

FIGURE 2 HAS ALWAYS BEEN A TOMBOY BUT AT 27 WILL COME OUT AS TRANS. THIS WILL BE CONFUSING AND A SOURCE OF ANXIETY.

FIGURE 1 HAS A GLUTEN INTOLERANCE.

FIGURE 2 LIKES DOGS MORE THAN CATS.

FIGURE 2'S BREATH TASTES SWEET AND WET AND PERFECT AND FIGURE 1'S CHEEKS START TO FEEL HOT.

FIGURE 1 IS AN ARTIST OF MOUNTING ACCLAIM. AT 36 FIGURE 1 WILL SAY TO THEIR THERAPIST THAT THEY HAVE ALWAYS USED ART TO DISSOCIATE FROM LIFE. THE THERAPIST WILL NOD GENTLY AND ASK HOW THIS MAKES FIGURE 1 FEEL, 'IT MAKES ME FEEL NOTHING' FIGURE 1 WILL SAY IN ANNOYANCE 'THAT'S OBVIOUSLY THE WHOLE POINT'. SHORTLY AFTER THIS SESSION FIGURE 1 WILL CHANGE THERAPISTS FOR THE 3ᴿᴰ TIME THAT YEAR.

SOON AFTER FIRST MEETING, FIGURE 1
AND FIGURE 2 SHARE A BEER ON FIGURE 1's
BALCONY, FIGURE 2 TALKS ABOUT BEING
AFRAID OF THE OCEAN, THEN FIGURE 1 TALKS
ABOUT HOW MUCH THEY LOVE BEING HIT
DURING SEX AND HOW IT'S HELPED THEM RECLAIM
AND REWIRE OLD EXPERIENCES OF ABUSE.

FIGURE 2 REALISES FOR THE FIRST
TIME HOW MUCH THEY LIKE
FIGURE 1.

FIGURE 2's FAVOURITE COLOUR IS BLUE.

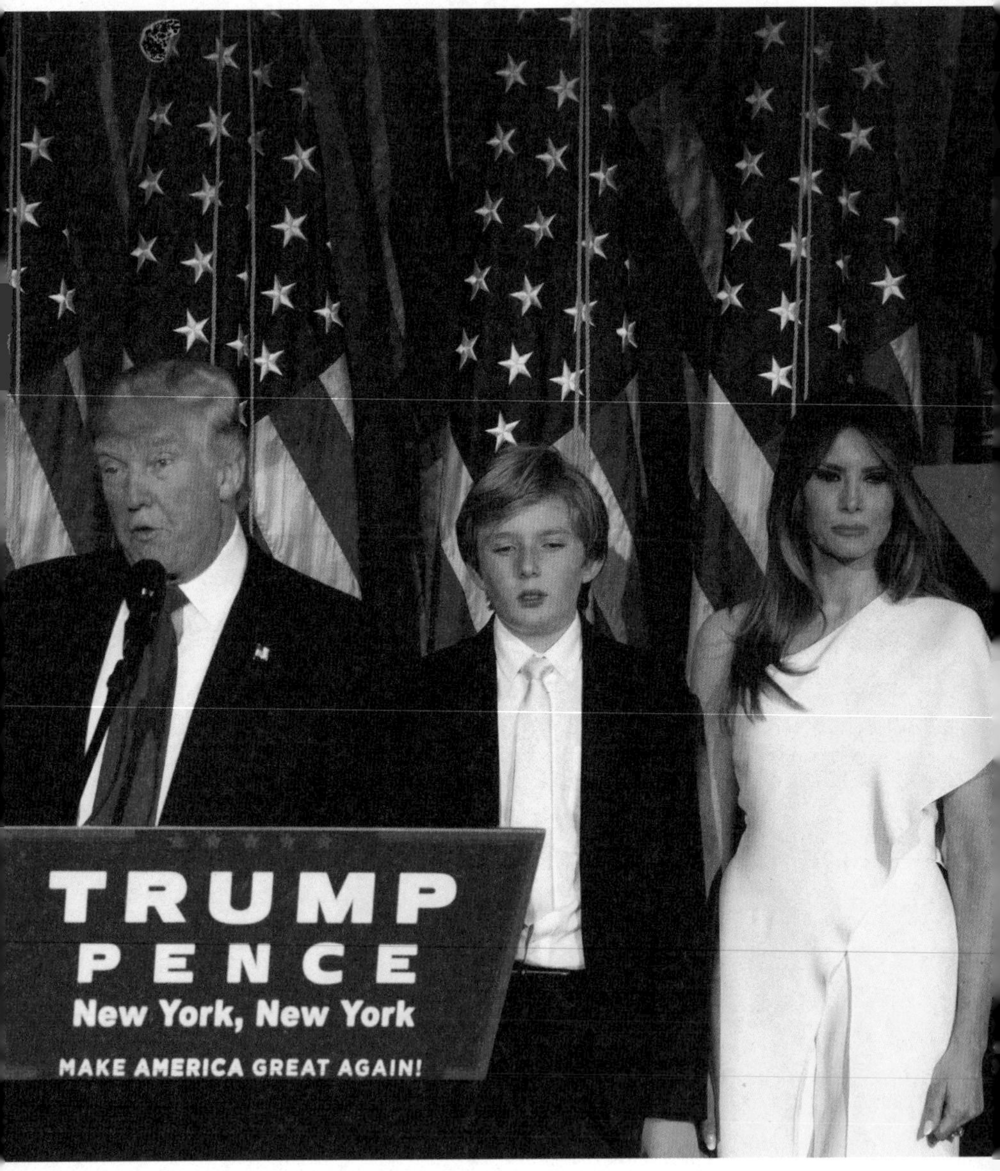
TRUMP
PENCE
New York, New York
MAKE AMERICA GREAT AGAIN!

I'VE SEEN THE FUTURE, BABY; IT IS MURDER

Tara Isabella Burton

When we woke up, we did not remember anything.

We'd emptied the minibar, I knew that much. A bottle of vodka was spinning on the bedside table. We'd tracked mud across the floor, and bits of stray bunting. Henry wore his swimsuit. It was fluorescent pink and emblazoned with five or six iterations of the American flag. I did not remember going swimming either.

Anyway, Henry had taken the bed.

I was on the floor. I did not know why. I had a vague, stiff sense that I was miserable, but I did not remember the reason for that either.

It was the knocking that woke us. I didn't move. The knocking got louder, and more insistent. I watched the ceiling fan spin like a pinwheel. There was tinsel caught in it.

'Christ, Susan,' said Henry, at last. 'Can't you make it stop?'

Of course, Henry could not see me. Henry was wearing his eye mask. He was very attached to this eye mask. He'd gotten it in the free toiletries bag in the business-class cabin of Cathay Pacific, on a trip to Hong Kong. He wore it every night. Sometimes he even wore it during sex.

When I got up, I fell over. I opened the door anyway.

It was the hotel clerk.

He was here to tell us that it was one o'clock in the afternoon. Checkout, he said, apologetically, was at eleven. If we didn't clear out, he said, he'd have to charge us for the extra night, and he didn't want to do that.

'Don't be ridiculous,' said Henry. He still had his eye mask on.

'I'm sorry, sir,' said the hotel clerk.

'Eight thirty,' Henry said again, like it was just a question of making himself clear.

'I'm truly, very sorry sir,' said the clerk. 'I'm afraid there wasn't a wake-up call on file for you.'

'Well of course there wasn't,' said Henry. 'Nobody uses hotel wake-up calls. Phones have rendered them *obsolescent*.' He got every syllable out correctly, and I wondered how.

Henry pushed his eye mask onto his forehead. He blinked very slowly. He reached, no less slowly, for his phone, which was not there.

The vodka bottle fell to the floor and shattered, right on top of the bunting I did not remember dragging in.

Henry stared, for a while, at the mess.

'Fuck,' said Henry.

We found Henry's phone, eventually. It was in the bottom of the hot tub by the deck. A woman in a bondage-themed bathing suit was passed out in the hot tub, and two girls with sequin-encrusted Uncle Sam hats were asleep on the deck chairs, and there, too, collapsed, where the infinity pool met the bay, were this young couple Henry and I had met the night before, who had asked us if we were together (he'd said no) and if we were Democrats (I'd said yes) and whether we'd wanted to share the pitcher of sangria they'd ordered (we'd said yes) and whether seeing all those damn Mexicans hanging around the city with nothing better to do than squeegee your windshield for tips had changed our minds, electorally speaking (we had not said anything).

Anyway, the phone was dead and there was no chance of saving it.

'Fucking Florida,' Henry said, and blinked.

W e missed our flight. We missed the next one, too, and the one after that, and also there was a thunderstorm brewing on the eastern seaboard, and severe fog in Atlanta, and a tornado watch in Charlotte, which meant that about half the flights to New York were canceled, and any flight with a connection was being rerouted.

The television screens in the lobby were all set to the news. They were all talking about the night before and *how* and *why* and *what could we have missed*. They were all on mute, and the figures were shadowy and strange. With us both so hungover and Henry screaming at his secretary on my phone ('There's *always* an extra seat,' he told me, 'you just have to put the fear of God into them, that's all'), the truth of it felt so alien, and removed, that if you had come up to me, that morning, and brought me a water and an aspirin and told me that Charlie Sheen had been elected president of the United States in his stead, I would probably have felt precisely the same way.

This is not your fault, I told myself. *You have not caused this.*

'Fuck it,' said Henry. 'We'll just drive.'

He tossed my phone back to me.

T he first time we'd fucked, we killed David Bowie.

I'd run into Henry on the street, that January. Ten years since college and Henry was unmistakable. He was paunchier, sure (I was thinner), but he wore the same bow ties, and the same tailored shirts, and the same blazers with the Lilly Pulitzer elbow patches that had made me refer to him, at school, as Patrick Bateman.

We had hated each other, but that was ten years before, and so we politely kissed on both cheeks.

'I've been following you,' said Henry.

He had a habit of grinning in such an obsequious way that you were never sure if he was serious.

'I read your writing. It's exactly what I expected of you.' I wrote on a variety of nebulous feminist issues for a midsize, online-only women's blog. 'Don't get me wrong. I mean that as a compliment.'

'You read *Misandry!* Really?'

'Of course I do.' Henry hadn't stopped grinning. 'Oppo research. Besides, men are terrible. I probably owe you a drink, don't I?'

Technically, I owed him a drink, since the last time I'd seen him I'd thrown a drink in his face (he'd used the word *cunt* in passing), but I wasn't about to press the point.

I let him buy me wine at the Campbell Apartment, which is a high-end speakeasy in Grand Central Station – it closed down later that summer – which I could never have afforded on my own. I told myself that this showed the extent to which I had come on in the world – that to sit, drinking wine, with a man I hated, smiling at his jokes and even parrying them, sometimes, was to be sophisticated, in some sense, or at least, in some sense, exciting.

He then took me to a speakeasy on the Lower East Side, where in order to get in you had to go upstairs through an employees-only entrance, and there he did not look at the cocktail menu, which was extensive, but instead ordered us two Old Fashioneds because, he said, the real test of a mixology bar was how well they did the classics.

'A condition of complete simplicity,' said Henry, smirking. 'Costing not less than everything.'

I made some noises indicating that I understood the reference, and Henry snorted, and said: '*Subtext*, young Susie, *the rest is silence*,' and although I should have been annoyed (that cannot be right; I *was* annoyed), somehow when he said: 'Before we go to a nightclub I should drop off my briefcase at my apartment,' which was in Gramercy, I agreed to go to his apartment, and then I did a few lines of coke with him, even though I'd only done coke once before, and then we fucked on his coffee table.

It was not very comfortable, but the appeal of it was that we did not like each other, and that it was on a coffee table, and so if it was not pleasurable it was, nonetheless, erotic.

Afterwards, he'd checked his phone.

'Bowie's dead.'

He kept scrolling through without looking at me.

'What?'

'David Bowie. He's dead.'

'Oh. Shit.' I had always liked David Bowie. When I was thirteen I saw *Labyrinth* for the first time and decreed he was probably the only man I would ever love. 'Was it an overdose or something?'

'No,' said Henry. 'He just got old.'

He smiled through the curl of his sneer.

'Do you want to know what I think?' He did not wait for me to answer. 'I think we caused it.' He had gotten up, already, and was scooping the powder off the coffee table into a little envelope. 'I think I always thought that. If you and I ever fucked – the four horsemen, right? We're causing the apocalypse – even now.'

He licked the back of the envelope to seal it.

'Aren't we special.'

We weren't. We were. Which is to say – I liked it. I do not know how to tell you why.

I could tell you I was bored that winter, which was true, and which was part of it. There was nothing particularly stimulating or new in writing about women's representation in the media, or condemning terrible men for anodyne offenses, or in politics that felt to me like Greek friezes: abstract, marble-hard and pure. I had a vague sense that things were Not Right, in a cosmic sense, and a far more immediate sense of personal comfort that ameliorated it, which is to say that I quite liked my life, stultifying as it was, and had no wish for any part of it to come to an end. I kept fucking Henry, and if you had told me that we had, really and unironically (not that we ever did anything unironically), killed David Bowie, I would have been rightfully horrified and guilty but also, beneath that, I would have felt a sickeningly erotic thrill: the same thrill I got from, for example, reading detailed Wikipedia accounts of deaths in horror movies I was too afraid to see.

Which is to say, when we killed Prince, the next time we slept together, some months after that, at an upscale hotel upstate (Henry liked to make a production of our meetings: they were always in hotels he seemed to have chosen for effect, and always – after that first time – out of town), I half believed that we had really done it.

The third time Henry and I had sex, we caused Brexit.
Henry kissed me, even though we never kissed.

'Look at the mess we've made.'

Henry got up.

'Did you know, young Susie, I've probably lost at least twenty thousand dollars. But it doesn't matter,' he said. He gargled with this blood-orange-flavored mouthwash he had brought all the way back with him from the Raffles Hotel in Singapore. He spat.

'Nothing matters,' he said.

He ordered a $300 bottle of champagne from room service (we were in New Orleans this time).

He tipped another hundred.

'Spend it while you can,' he told the waiter. 'Soon we'll all be hoarding metal scraps and scrounging for the gold fillings in our teeth.'

He poured me a glass. He toasted me.

'When the revolution comes,' said Henry, 'that's when we'll be tested – for real, I mean. That's when men will have to be men again – put that in one of your articles.'

Henry frequently told me I should put him in my articles. He'd go on record, he said, as an *expert source, a professional performer of straight white male privilege*. He would be memorialized.

'I can see it now. "It Happened to Me: My Finance-Bro-Fuck Buddy and I Survived the Post-Brexit Global Meltdown Through Strategically Implemented Cannibalism."'

I laughed.

It was ridiculous, of course. I knew that. Henry was ridiculous. But the champagne, or the sex, had made me giddy, and the transgression of listening to him, in all his unapologetic offense, had not yet worn off.

S o when Henry texted me, in late October – *want to watch the season finale of America with me?* – from the Standard Hotel in Miami, I only pretended to hesitate. He had not texted me in two months, and in that time I had half-heartedly started one or two book proposals for solemn but career-enhancing essay collections about female representation on television sitcoms and also what it meant to be a *fearless woman*. In that time, too, I had acquired one or two boyfriends who were assiduous, and communicative, and who always made sure I came.

Let's pop the popcorn, I said.

I'm sure you'll enjoy it, said Henry. *Would our first woman president turn you on?*

Careful, I said. *We might turn it the other way.*

From your mouth to God's ears, said Henry.

Spoiler alert, said Henry. *The house always wins.*

N ow, of course, we did not cause it. I mean, Henry wasn't even awake for it.

We dressed for dinner and I wore the Agent Provocateur underwear that I'd spent my latest paycheck on, and thigh-high stockings which took me twenty minutes to attach to the suspenders, and which after twenty minutes I still had not properly affixed, and also stilettos I could not walk in. I felt that I was performing the kind of girl that Henry liked to pretend he liked, who was blonde and very thin and went to SoulCycle (I mean, I also went to SoulCycle), and who pouted underneath dark sunglasses, and who was urbane, and also very chill about things like other women and anal sex. I was, I felt, performing Miami too; I was tacky and glamorous and erotic and not myself and I did not like this vision of not-myself, exactly, but I liked that I was capable of putting it on, with at least some degree of ease, and that I would take it off as soon as the election was over and I went back to my proper life in New York. It made me feel powerful. It made me feel unlike other women, who, I assumed, only had one self.

We sat by the pool and we made friends and we talked politics with strangers and we drank sangria and we took some Xanax and we drank frosé, which is what you get when you make a slushie out of frozen rosé wine, and we took some more Xanax to calm our nerves, even though we had nothing to be nervous about, even though the first woman president was going to be elected in a matter of hours, and Henry said *I guess this is one point for Susie* and I pulled nervously at where my stockings met my suspenders, since I had twisted the garters and the hooks were digging into the back of my thighs, and we hadn't had sex yet so I hadn't had an opportunity to take them off, and then we drank Old Fashioneds and took another Xanax, and then we had sex, and then in the hotel lobby a drag queen in a pantsuit and a drag king wearing orange bronzer were having a Political Trivia contest, and I won a round of shots by correctly naming all the candidates' children, and things were going so well Henry even had me sit on his lap, and kissed my shoulder, which is just another thing that we never did, and then the Xanax kicked in and Henry said *I'm bored, I'm going to go take a nap, wake me in an hour*, and so I waited alone, watching the results at the hotel bar, buying strangers gin and tonics on the tab Henry had started, and felt sophisticated and brazen, drunkenly saying things to strangers like *oh, Henry, no, we aren't dating, I can't stand him, we're just fucking, anyway, as one does; we killed Prince*, except in that hour we lost Florida, and so I ran back to the room and shook Henry awake and he said *five more minutes* and I said *we've lost Florida* and Henry said *who cares about Florida* and I shook him again and he said *for Christ's sake, Susie, I'll deal with it in the morning* and I started to cry and he said *go to bed it won't affect you anyway* and I could not stay in there so I went outside to the pool to sob (I may have thrown his phone into the hot tub, where the couple with whom we had shared the sangria were fucking a celebratory fuck) and so I saw the fate of the world decided, alone.

'Eighteen hours to New York,' said Henry. He swung the car keys around his fingers. 'You'd better take a Modafinil.'

Henry had rented a Porsche. It was a hideous fire-truck shade of red, a *fuck-you car*, Henry said, from a classic-car club where his father had an account.

'*Damyata*,' said Henry, as we got in. 'The Porsche responded/ Gaily, to the hand expert . . . your heart would have responded/Gaily, when invited, beating obedient/To controlling hands.'

He grimaced at me, or else it was a grin.

'Cheer up, Susie,' he said. 'When the barbarians come knocking, we'll at least be able to outrace them.'

The water was gray. The fog was gray. Gray, too, was the knife's edge where the bay met the sky. On the radio, the commentators all passed judgment on the news, and adjudicated about whether it was the emails that had done it, or the letter, or the leaks, or whether it was about Russia or white people or atavism ('It's always atavism,' said Henry), and then they started playing the victory speech, and words were so much realer than the pictures had been, and when I heard his voice I became sick and rudderlessly angry once again.

Tremendous potential. I've gotten to know our country so well. Tremendous potential. It's going to be a beautiful thing.

Henry looked over at me. He gave me a blithe, quizzical smile.

'Not a fan?'

I didn't say anything. My tongue was fat in my mouth. I was too parched, and too sick, to speak. Even if I could speak, I had nothing I could say.

'Are we triggered, young Susie?'

It was the sort of joke that was a joke, between us, or had been, like when he ordered for me at dinner, or called me a cunt in bed.

'It's fine,' I said. 'I just don't like listening to him.'

'Short-fingered vulgarian. That's what Graydon Carter called him.' Henry sped up a little more. 'My father has him to dinner, you know. Graydon Carter, I mean. Obviously. We're not animals.'

'Good for you.'

Even the palm trees looked sick. They were all influenza yellow.

'Cheer up,' said Henry. 'We'll listen to something else.'

He grabbed my phone, plugged it in, fiddled with Spotify awhile.

Trumpets blared through the speakers.

'Are you serious?'

It was the prelude to Wagner's *Tristan und Isolde*. Henry had a thing about Wagner. It worried his father, he said, which was another thing that Henry found funny, except Henry maintained it was just about the music and the spectacle.

'Not you too,' he said. '*Really*, Susie.'

He poked me.

'It's not like I'm wearing Hugo Boss,' said Henry.

He turned the music up louder.

'Come on, Susie, everyone in Brooklyn has a fashy haircut now . . .'

He wanted me to say something, or do something, and I did not know what it was, and it made me angry, because Henry so rarely wanted anything from me at all, and the one time he had given me power I did not know what to do with it.

I just kept looking out the window, saying nothing, biting my lip, blinking back tears, trying to put my reeling into words.

Then Henry sped up. It was just a little bit, at first, enough for me to think he was trying to dodge somebody's slow-moving grandpa.

Then a little bit faster.

Then Henry revved the engine, loud and sharp enough to jerk me forward, and so loud some guy shouted *asshole* at us from thirty paces behind.

Fast enough to dredge up vomit from the back of my throat.

We did ninety. Henry kept his eyes on the road. His mouth was a slow, glazed, gaping smile.

We did ninety-five. The speedometer trembled higher.

It struck me, then, that Henry was waiting for me to stop him, that it would give him pleasure if I shouted at him, and I did not want to give him the satisfaction of shouting at him, since my silence was the only resource I had, and because he wanted me to I did not, even though we were at one hundred now, going so fast and so rashly that I thought we *would* surely crash, we would crash, there was no way we could keep going like this and *not* crash, and I stared straight ahead and thought *fine, let us crash*, and maybe it's because if you're going to crash your car you might as well do it in an ugly Porsche, blasting Wagner, and maybe it's just because I was hungover, and sick, and the world was ending, and I just didn't have the energy to care about what was coming next, and either way I wanted us to crash.

We made it all the way to one-ten before Henry slammed on the brakes.

We both jerked against the dashboard. My stockings, still twisted on the garters, drew blood at the back of my thighs.

Henry looked, I thought, like a crash-test dummy.

He turned to me.

'Jesus,' he said. He sounded disappointed. 'You really *are* mad at me, aren't you?'

I didn't say anything.

'I don't know what you're so angry about,' he said. 'I voted for her.'

I had never asked. I had assumed. Everything that offended me about Henry I had hoped was disingenuous; his irony, too, had been part of what attracted me to him. I had never imagined he was responsible, in any electoral way, for the outcome.

Still, I could not look at him.

'I'm not angry at you,' I said, even though this was clearly a lie.

'I've been reading *FiveThirtyEight*,' said Henry. 'It's your fault, apparently. *White women's tears.*' He seemed to enjoy this, too.

'It's not funny,' I said.

'It's not *not* funny,' said Henry. 'Besides, he won't be able to do anything. There are people around him who will make sure of that. He'll be out by springtime, probably. And even if he isn't, it's not like they'll let him make decisions.'

He snorted.

'Isn't that the reassuring thing about patriarchy, young Susie? You learn that the house always, always wins.'

Finally, Henry sighed.

'You know,' he said. 'For a man of the Upper East Side, I must confess I'm remarkably bad at holding my Xanax.'

It was the closest he'd ever come to apologizing to me for anything.

'Anyway,' said Henry, 'you're the writer. If one of us was going to bear witness to America jumping the shark, it might as well be you. Chronicle the slow, painful decay of straight white men like me?'

He punched me, lightly, on the shoulder, and I was not as angry as I was, or, at least, should have been.

'It Happened to Me,' I said, at last. 'I Spent Election Night 2016 in Miami on Benzos with My Finance-Bro-Fuck Buddy.'

Wagner was still blaring on the stereo, and we were still speeding down the highway in that ridiculous Porsche, and now that we were not listening to the news it felt, again, as it had always felt with us, and the real world did not exist, and this was all a great and cosmic joke, being played out by the universe specifically for our benefit, and nothing real would ever really happen. When the world ended, it would be like the twilight of the gods, and nothing like real life.

'Don't tell them I slept through it,' said Henry.

At nightfall we stopped at an Econo Lodge near Asheville. We had another eight hours to go, but Henry and I were both tired, and neither of us wanted to drive through the night.

'Besides,' said Henry, 'I want to see something of the Real America.'

He had parked his Porsche right outside our room, which was on the ground floor. There were cigarette burns on the comforter.

'*This?*' Henry said, taking out hand sanitizer (this one was from the Plaza Athénée in Paris). '*This* is what we underestimated?'

It was less a terrible motel room than a Hollywood film set of a terrible motel room. The hair dryer didn't work and the television wires were frayed.

Henry plugged in the coffee maker.

The fuse blew in a sad, impotent spark.

Henry looked at me with the fuse in his hand.

I looked back at him.

I do not know which one of us started laughing first, but in a moment we were together in it, hacking so bleakly, punctuating our hysterics with coughs first intermittent then overwhelming, and we laughed so hard, staring at one another, at the fuse and the motel and the missed flights and the election and the whole cataclysmic strangeness of the world that, for a moment, I forgot that I blamed him for everything.

'Well,' said Henry, 'I suppose we can't do any *more* damage, now?'

He touched my shoulder so lightly. And the truth is: I loved the feeling of it.

'I mean,' said Henry, 'how much worse can it get?'

He kissed me.

It was like a real kiss, the way he kissed me then, real enough that I stepped back and let my knees buckle the way they do in films, real enough that I opened my lips, only then he pushed me away and turned me around and pushed me over the bed, the way he always had done, and pushed my underwear to one side and called me a cunt, and fucked me from behind, as joylessly and as mechanically as if he were coming into his hand.

I didn't say anything.

I can't tell you why.

Henry finished and pulled out. He grabbed the hand sanitizer.

'You know your garters are twisted, right?'

He was already gargling blood-orange into the sink.

I am not an idiot. I knew the rules. I am not a romantic, and I am enough of a feminist to safeguard my own agency and enough of a hypocrite to like being called a cunt, and I had asked for this, all of this. I knew what Henry was but in that moment I wanted him to be himself, but also somebody else.

I stood there, at the side of the bed, pulling my garters up.

Henry put on his eye mask.

'We should get some sleep,' he said. 'I have a lunch meeting in New York at noon.'

He lay there, on the bed, with his mask on.

S o I did a stupid thing. I turned the television on. I turned it on to MSNBC.

Rachel Maddow was talking about the victory speech. They were playing it, over and over, and analyzing different sections of it, and a panel of experts was adjudicating whether he had, in fact, been rendered presidential by the office entrusted to him, and Henry did not stir or make a sound.

So I turned the volume up as loud as it would go.

'Jesus, Susie, would you turn that down?'

I felt the crunch of power, making him talk.

'Jesus, Susie – you've probably woken all the neighbors.'

'Fuck the neighbors,' I said. Then: 'They probably voted for him. They should have to live with it.'

'Susie.'

'Don't you *care*?' I said.

A coup was coming, I said. Hadn't he thought of that? Wasn't there going to be an assault on our civil liberties, and also, also, had he thought of this, if he'd knocked me up, just now, fucking me, then how would he like it if I weren't able to get an abortion, what would he think of that?

'That's ridiculous,' said Henry. 'You have an IUD in. Plus, you'd find out in January, anyway, and he's not going to do a thing by then, and, anyway, there's nothing you can do about it now.'

I don't remember what I shouted about next. I think it was the widows, and orphans, and refugees, and the tired and the weak and the poor and the young, and every single thing I said was true, and sincere, and still the shameful truth of it was that all I wanted was for him to look at me.

'It's the end of the fucking world, Henry!'

'Then put the end of the world on headphones.'

'You're a fucking asshole.'

They were playing the victory speech again.

Get over here, Reince. Boy oh boy oh boy. It's about time you did this, Reince. My God. Say a few words. No, come on, say something.

'I didn't even *vote* because of you!'

O f course I'd meant to. What kind of imbecile would not mean to? It's just that the flight to Miami had been so early, that day. It's just that I'd planned to go, on my way to the airport, but then I'd overslept and I was a New York resident, after all, and New York was going to go blue no matter what I did, so it did not really matter if I voted or not, and it *had* not mattered if I voted or not, since we'd won the popular vote even without me, and we'd lose the electoral college, even without me, and it was not my fault and I had not caused the apocalypse, not by sleeping with Henry and not by coming to Miami to sleep with Henry and not even by not voting, because I was coming to Miami to sleep with Henry, it was not my fault, and I was not a bad person, and nothing I had done could condemn me, in a court of law or maybe even the celestial kind, but I hated myself, anyway, because what kind of person cares whether a man is in love with her, at a time like this, and what kind of person secretly hopes the world will blow up at her feet, just to make her feel less bored, or less unenchanted, or less alone?

'That's not my problem,' said Henry, and he was right.

He pulled off his mask.

'I'm going for a smoke,' he said.

I did not stop him.

I heard him a few minutes later.

A couple of kids were taking selfies with the Porsche. They were college kids, if that – white, in sweatshirts, clearly drunk, probably a bit stoned.

'Hey!' Henry was shouting. 'I'll have you know that's a *vintage air-cooled Porsche.*'

'Sure,' said one of the kids.

'I *said*,' Henry took another step nearer, 'that's a motherfucking *vintage air-cooled Porsche*.'

'So?' said another kid. 'What the hell do you want me to do about it?'

'What I *want*,' said Henry, 'is for you to step away from my *vintage air-cooled Porsche*.'

It was the first time I had ever seen him genuinely upset about anything.

It wasn't even his car.

'One day. Is that all it fucking takes?'

The kids were looking at him like he was crazy.

'Is it a free-for-all now, is that it?'

I opened the door.

'Just let them have their fun, Henry,' I said. 'They're just kids – come on. They just want to take some selfies.'

Henry wasn't listening to me.

'You get your guy in and now you think you just *run* the place, is that it?'

His laugh sounded like a hiccup.

'You're fucking trash – all of you!'

I don't know what Henry thought he was doing. It was, I thought, impossible for him to have seriously considered that he might have a chance against them. There were four of them, and he barely came up to the shortest one's chin. He wasn't even in shape.

But he punched one of them, anyway.

It went exactly the way you'd expect.

Two of them held Henry down. A third pummeled him. They kicked him in the stomach and punched him in the face until he was spitting blood onto the parking lot.

They hit him until he wheezed, and sobbed, and then one of them called him a little bitch and kicked him in the balls.

They beat up the Porsche, for good measure.

They put a dent in the front door and another in the back. They smashed the glass in the back seat.

They ran off.

Henry didn't even look up.

He just lay there, sobbing.

I brought him inside. He didn't say anything. He stared straight ahead, shaking. I didn't have rubbing alcohol but I ministered to his wounds with his hand sanitizer, and made him gargle out the blood with his orange Raffles mouthwash, and put the eye mask over his forehead.

'You don't understand,' Henry kept saying. 'You don't understand.'

He swallowed.

He didn't even blink.

'It's not my account. It's not mine.'

'What are you talking about?'

'The car. The – the *Porsche*. It's not my fucking *account*.'

It was his father's.

'We'll call him in the morning,' I said. 'You'll tell him what happened. It's not your fault.'

It was, of course, but that part, I thought, we could leave out.

'You don't understand. My father –'

Henry shook his head. He kept on shaking it, so that his refusal morphed into a shiver.

'Fucking barbarians at the gate,' he said. 'It's a fucking disgrace.'

Then: 'What gives them the right –'

He coughed up blood into his hand.

'What gives anyone the fucking *right* ... ?'

He wiped blood onto the comforter.

'*Cunts*,' said Henry.

We stayed up all night. We did not talk. We did not touch each other. We just remained, straight-backed, alongside one another, watching the news.

In the morning, Henry called his father.

He did not do this in front of me. He went outside into the parking lot, and closed the door tightly behind him, and although I could not hear him, through the blinders I could see him shouting, and pacing around the destroyed Porsche, and kicking it.

He was very calm, coming back inside.

'The company's going to send someone,' he said. 'There are very specialized repairs.' He grimaced, again, that grimace that was also a grin. 'I'll drop it off at the Asheville airport and fly from there. My – he's getting me a flight.'

He swallowed.

'The old man should be grateful,' he said. 'When – when the war comes, I'm going to carry him out of New York on my back. Like Aeneas carrying Anchises. You know that one, right?'

We were in the same Latin class. I reminded him of this.

'Right you are,' he said. 'Fragments against the ruin. Of course – I'm taking up CrossFit, when I get back. That's one for your article, Susie, isn't it? "It Happened to Me: I Dated a CrossFit Bro at the Apocalypse."'

'I'm not going to write that,' I said.

'Why not? *Misandry!* would love it.'

'I'm quitting *Misandry!*' I said.

'Why? It was funny.'

'It's obsolescent,' I said.

That made him laugh.

'So what are you going to do now?' he said. 'Take up arms?'

'Maybe,' I said.

'Give me your passport number,' said Henry. 'He'll get you a flight, too.'

'It's okay,' I said. 'I'll take the bus.'

'Nobody takes the fucking bus.'

'I'll be fine,' I said. 'I like the bus. It's interesting. I get to watch people.'

He shrugged. 'Women,' he said. 'You're all enigmas. Am I right?'

I told Henry he had never been right about anything in his life. He seemed to like that.

Henry drove off, blasting *Tristan und Isolde* through the broken back window.

I stood there, after him, watching his absence, and marveling at what a strange and what a terrible thing we had done.

I thought, for a while, about what I would say, if I ever had children, or grandchildren, and their sixth-grade social-studies teacher gave them assignments much as I had gotten, asking my parents where they had been when JFK was shot.

I thought, at first, that I would lie, and tell them that I had been at a protest, or a rally, that I had been at a get-out-the-vote initiative, although I supposed that the possibility of children or grandchildren was remote for me for a variety of reasons, which was partly to do with the state of the world and partly to do with my own mental and financial health, and I supposed that for all I knew nobody would be having children or grandchildren in a generation's time, and also for all I knew Henry was right and nothing much would change and my children and grandchildren would have better things to do than ask me about a day that was, in the great cosmic scheme of things, just like any other, but I came to the conclusion, as I walked down the highway, toward the bus stop that would lead me into town, that if somebody did ask me what I had done, I would tell them about the red Porsche, and about the Wagner, and the eye mask, although I do not think I come out very well in it, no better, probably, than Henry, but the one thing I have going for me is that I do not have to be disingenuous, if I do not want to be, and it would be disingenuous to say anything else. ∎

Fiona Benson

Zeus

days I talked with Zeus
I ate only ice
felt the blood trouble and burn
under my skin

found blisters
on the soft parts
of my body

bulletproof glass
and a speakerphone between us
and still I wasn't safe

thunder moved in my brain
tissue-crease
haemorrhage

I kept the dictaphone running
it recorded nothing
but my own voice
vulcanized and screaming
you won't get away with this

[archives]

Zeus on parole:

NO FUN
THIS ANKLEBAND
TAZERS ME
EVERY TIME
I BRUSH THE BOUNDS
AND YET IT IS
SHALL WE SAY
EROTIC?
ITS SUDDEN CURSE
ITS THRILL

[surveillance: bull kneeling]

not there   dusk like a bruise   its yellow air
not there yet   some difficulty   in transmission
the near trees thrashing   and that thickening,
how it stirs   at the edge of the field   milk cows backed
against the furthest stile   stamping their hooves
like epileptics   drumming their heels   on the floor
nostrils frothing   the scorched white smell   of myrrh –
not there still   charcoal blur   manifesting
like a storm out at sea   bull on its knees   was it
was it flies?   staggers up   white bull smirched
lightning in his horns   phallus scarlet   and engorged
thunder crackles   on his suede   as he bellows
and the ground gapes   to the underworld   and all the dead
scream out   girl walking   by the river
drops her flowers and her phone   turns   starts to run

[archives]

The day Zeus came to the safe house
and shoved a sawn-off shotgun
through the letter box   calling softly
like he was calling to the cats
that terrible croon, *HEY HONEYS
I'M HOME*

Had them kettled for hours.
Oh yes they were mightily changed.
Maddened, fuguing. Dissolved to rivers,
shaking like trees in a hurricane.
Some of them damaged in their entrails,
two thrown from high windows;
impossible to save.

[Callisto]

Split urethra, fistula, stitched rectum.
Infant removed *for its own protection.*
Her breasts are searing bags of milk,
her shirt is soaked. She will not talk.
Her mother takes her home, coaxes her to eat,
roasts chicken with potatoes, herbs and salts the skins.
Callisto picks the carcass clean, moves on –
pork chops, dumplings, chocolate rolls,
past repletion, through to the distended gullet,
forced stomach, goose with a funnel down its throat
and the grain shovelled in with a scoop,
beak tied shut, liver corrupt.
She holds herself down, clamps her mouth,
piles on flesh like upholstery,
does violence to herself, cuts, infected sores,
squats to shit does not wipe does not wash
her hair down her back in a matted clump,
her hunch and look-away demeanour delivering her over
onto all fours, patchy fur, hardened claws.
Her mother searches in the dark –
every doorway and underpass.

Finds her daughter mite-ridden and stubborn.
Callisto I love you come home.
Cornered by a ranger one morning Callisto
rakes at the air with her paws, is chased out of town
with tranq guns and flares, their falling coals like meteors.
But there is pleasure in the woods –
the sun shining amber on her fur,
the teeming world of the river as she hunts headlong
after fish, or shins up a tree tracking bees
and bites through the sugared wax crust
to the golden ooze of the honey. She grooms herself
with a rasped tongue, heaving her body over
to reach her belly. There are moments in her cave
when she almost feels safe, and sleeps to dream
of the cub who mewed at her briefly before he was taken;
his eyes swollen shut from the pressure of birth,
his small blind face searching for her voice,
his kicking legs and his tiny fists waving.
Bundled out of the room. Perfect human.
Her voice, when she calls for him,
is the voice of her own mother, weeping.
Go ahead, Zeus. Constellate this.

[screenplay]

Zeus rattling his tin cup
on the bars of his cell
>   *cut*
Zeus in the exercise yard
looking up through rain
his upturned face, his smile
>   *cut*
Zeus who can walk between raindrops
without getting wet
who can pass through the vaults
and walls of this prison
as if they were air
who could pour himself
between the atoms.
You've got to ask
why he's here?
HERA.

[surveillance]

Zeus watching carp in the hospital pond
on Zenuphlate, Zemperon X, Prozac, sedatives.
Getting an erection through the haze
shifting back and forth,
fidgeting with his slacks,
distressed.
The psych nurse brings pills
in a doll-sized paper cup.
These are for you Zeus.
Hold out your tongue.
What nymphs go dancing in your brain,
what tortures?
I WILL RAPE A CHILD WITH AN IMPLEMENT
AND THAT IMPLEMENT WILL BE SWAN.

Debra Gwartney and her mother, 1957
Courtesy of the author

ABSCESSED TOOTH

Debra Gwartney

Near the end of the 1970s, my parents drove across the state of Idaho for Parents' Weekend at the university where I was a sophomore. They picked me up at my house and we headed toward campus. There would be a picnic and music on the expansive lawn. The sun was shining, and the brown snow heaped by the side of the roads during the winter had finally melted into pale grass. As we drove, my mother asked me about my classes, my father wondered when I'd start looking for a summer job. They discussed where to park. Chatter like that, with none of us mentioning the five days I'd spent in the hospital some months earlier after a botched abortion.

As we got ready to leave the car, I felt I had to bring it up. I hadn't seen them since before the hospital stay; they hadn't asked me once how I was faring and I was bothered by that. And yet the words I managed to get out as we drove were innocuous. Something like: 'now that I feel better'. I don't recall the context exactly. 'I can stay up later now that I feel better', a sentence just that mundane which caused my mother to stiffen in her seat, the ropy muscle in her neck taut, her hands stacked in her lap so that her narrow gold wedding band popped from the surface of her finger. My father tapped the turn signal and looked elsewhere, anywhere. That was the end of it.

Too bad, because I had questions for them. I have questions for them now, forty years later. Such as: what my mother, who answered the phone, was told about their eldest child's predicament. I wonder if they were troubled to hear I'd been admitted to a hospital in another state. As for me, I remember little. A white hallway, a crackling voice over a speaker calling for physicians, a nurse fiddling with the IV in my arm and, once, my own doctor standing at the edge of the bed. He'd been there other days, no doubt, but this is my single recollection of him, the way he kept his hands in his white coat and told me that he'd approved a call to my parents to settle insurance matters. I remember that.

I also remember leaving the hospital. Sitting in a wheelchair at the glass sliding doors in the wrinkled clothes I'd had on when I was brought to the emergency room, the dried blood in my underwear, my pants itchy against my thighs and, oddly, the soles of my feet itching too. I waited for my boyfriend to pull up in his blue truck and get me back to college, an hour's drive through rolling pea and lentil farmland and curves of lodgepole pine. I thought I could still be the girl I'd been before all of this. I still believed that was possible.

A nurse waited with me for my boyfriend's arrival. Maybe I recognized her as one of those who'd thumped on the IV line and stuck a thermometer in my mouth before disappearing again into the long white hallway. She said how surprised she was that I'd had no visitors over the week, a pretty girl like me, a pretty blond college girl like me. But I hadn't expected friends, or boyfriend, nor did I believe I'd wake up to find either parent in my room, even after they'd been told where I was.

I did manage to convince myself, back then when I was nineteen, that I'd been put at the end of the hallway at my parents' bidding. They preferred I stay hidden away. Mine was the last door before the exit that led outside and in my memory no one except nurses walked by or peeked in. These nurses turned knobs on the blinking machine and stuck needles into junctures of tube, and maybe around the second day I began to imagine that, oh yes, right, my father had arranged something else, too. My drug-addled mind was certain my mother had urged him on – a single shot into the IV bag, just toxic enough that it would enter my system a drop at a time and I'd soon fall asleep and drift away. My parents could then tell their friends a sad story about a wildfire infection through my body, cause unknown and caught too late. I lay in bed and waited for that final drip to begin.

About seven years before, my grandmother had died – a death caused by an abscessed tooth that actually had spread like fire through her blood – her broken mind tumbled her into silence. She moved into a space without language that I believe in some ways she'd aimed for most of her life – she no longer had to keep explaining, even to herself, why she had forged on for so long. But before she stopped speaking completely, my grandmother hung on to a few last statements, platitudes that were reminders to herself and to us of who she'd been. One sentence she often repeated near the end was this: Into every life some rain must fall.

I was the eldest of my parents' four children. Then I was the mother of four girls, and one day, when those children were little, a woman named Ella asked me to meet her at the airport in our town. She was my mother's closest childhood friend and she said her layover would give us a chance to catch up. Ella watched me with my daughters that afternoon, the oldest two running around the waiting area, the younger two in my lap. 'I wonder when,' she said, reaching over to touch my arm as if to wake me up, 'you'll all stop trying to replace your grandmother's babies.'

My grandmother's four babies, she meant: three boys and a girl, each of whom died at birth, or shortly after.

As a girl I knew the rule, even though it was unspoken: never talk about the babies around our grandmother; do not ask about her children buried under a headstone with its epitaph, BUDDED ON EARTH TO BLOOM IN HEAVEN. I understood that in my family it was a failure to speak of procreative failure. The making of babies was a complicated matter, often ill-timed, ill-executed, as easily the cause of sorrow as joy, and words about these ruined events would weaken us, rob us of fortitude. Best for you, if you were a woman, to keep such troubles to yourself.

My mother kept her troubles to herself, though she did say to me a few times, in fits of anger, that she'd fought a whole town so that I could live. I was a child when I first heard her proclamation, and I pictured my mother at the end of Main Street, there at the turnoff to Highway 20, using a stick in her hand to wave off the people chasing her down. Were my grandmothers in that crowd? My great-aunts? My cousins? The girl who served milk and donuts at Wally's Cafe or Ikey, who cut our hair?

Later I realized, of course, that few people in town were concerned about whether or not I'd survive. My mother's fight back then was not about if I'd live, but about where. I understood, too, that it wasn't all that unusual for teenage girls in rural Idaho to show up pregnant: no big deal. My grandparents had hired an attorney to draw up adoption papers so that I could be taken away to a ranching family or handed off to a barren couple in Boise. That was the plan. My seventeen-year-old mother and sixteen-year-old father could get back to things, return to school, and never again speak of their accident.

They didn't speak of it again. To this day, what I know about my beginnings I've pieced together myself: how my father picked up my mother one day to drive her to the courthouse, less than a hundred yards from my grandparents' front door. The justice of the peace married them with (I'm imagining here) the smell of my grandmother's fried elk steaks wafting in the window. A month later I was born.

While my mother's mother lay dying, I held her paper-thin hand and thought about apologizing for spoiling her daughter's future. I could tell her I was sorry that my grandparents' one surviving child had gone wrong by bearing a child of her own too soon, but I said nothing. Instead, my sister came in the room and we crawled into bed with our grandmother, one on each side. We sang 'You Are My Sunshine', because that's the song she'd sung to us. I said, 'Into every life some rain must fall,' into her ear, thinking she might hear that sentence over the hum and clang in the room and accept it as a release. Then my sister whispered into our grandmother's cloud of white hair, 'You can go now. Your babies are waiting for you.' Even at the very end those words rattled me – I sat up and stared at my sister. 'Don't you know we are never to speak about the dead children?'

In my sophomore year of college, in the bleak of winter, this same sister had come for a weekend visit to campus with a group from her high school. She had only a few hours to see me and I was glad for it, because my boyfriend had, earlier that week on an afternoon free of classes, driven me across the state border to a clinic in Washington State where, for $250, I could legally end my pregnancy. The nurse who handed me a gown and a locker key told me, 'No big deal.' A half-hour in a dank room, ten minutes or so with a doctor, cramping like a bad period. I might be moody for a few days due to jumbled hormones. And she was right that afterward I wanted to see no one, grateful for the windy drive from the clinic back to our college. I could stare out the window at the fallow fields, the skim of snow across bare earth, and say nothing.

On my sister's last night on campus, which was four days after my abortion, I agreed to go out to dinner with her to a tiny cafe downtown that was too expensive, and yet distant enough from the garbage pail full of bloody pads in my room, the wrinkled sheets of my bed, that I could act like the sister she knew. A waitress had brought our sodas when I felt an anvil drop from my head to my feet. That was the sensation, anyway, too heavy and too immediate. My sister said, 'What's wrong? You're so white.' I told her I'd probably caught the flu; it was going around. I left her to pay the bill and find her way back to the dorm where she was staying. I walked to my own house in the cold dark thinking, *Whatever this is could kill me,* a statement in line with my penchant for melodrama, except it held none of the regular thrill of hyperbole but instead a thud of truth.

I was in my boyfriend's truck soon after that, swinging through

DEBRA GWARTNEY

mountain curves and the straightaways through peas and lentils to the clinic again – how we decided to return to the original scene, I don't recall. What he told my sister, I don't know. I don't know if she called to check on me, or to say goodbye, or if she went home to tell my parents I was sick. In some ways, I've spent forty years avoiding my sister so the subject won't come up – though now that I think about it, I stopped worrying about such a conversation a long time ago. The not-talking has simply become comfortable. The soothing habit of omission. Silence allows me to pretend that this happened to someone else a long time ago, and not to me.

When my boyfriend and I reached the emergency room next to the clinic, I was unconscious across the front seat, bleeding down my legs. I was moved to a table and the same doctor I had seen four days earlier met us there. I recognized him when I came around long enough to notice the cold of the steel against my skin and this physician between my yawning legs shouting at the nurses for the right instruments. The next time I saw him, he was standing at my bed. 'They had to be told,' he said about my parents.

No one asked me where I'd been when I returned to school. A friend made up a bed for me in the basement of my house, away from my roommates, but didn't inquire about what had gone wrong or why I'd been away for nearly a week. It was hard, but right when I thought it was all too hard, I surprised myself by getting well. It didn't hurt anymore to breathe. Spring arrived, and suddenly Parents' Weekend was in the past, my mother and father returned to their home with the unspoken agreement between us that there would be no conversation about what had happened to me.

During this time of recuperation, I happened to hear two girls explain why they'd been away from campus for several days. One said she'd had an abscessed tooth and went to her parents' house to recover. The other said that she, too, had left because of an abscessed tooth. So odd, I thought. What were the chances? And then, not long after, yet another girl spoke of an abscessed tooth as her reason for a brief departure from school, and I thought: Oh. The others had learned a mutual code, a shared signal that had somehow failed to reach me. I stood by as these girls explained their trouble to each other swiftly, easily; I watched how they let each other pass in relative peace and sisterhood, while I had missed it. I had remained alone, and let my trouble fester and boil.

At the end of college I married the boy who'd made me pregnant – I thought back then, *Who else would take me?* Maybe he believed the same. We went on to have four daughters together. Four children to replace my grandmother's dead babies? I'm not so sure about that. Though maybe. Four daughters to fill a certain hole in me is probably closer to the truth. Because back when I was still a child myself, a girl steeped in the way things were done in my family, with no ability to imagine it differently, I spent five days alone at the end of a hallway in a hospital. More alone than I have been again.

And until this moment, I have spoken about it to no one. ■

'A writer to go travelling with on the journey called life . . . wild and funny, questioning and true'
Jeanette Winterson

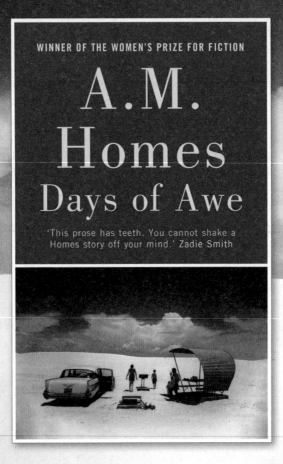

WINNER OF THE WOMEN'S PRIZE FOR FICTION

A.M. Homes
Days of Awe

'This prose has teeth. You cannot shake a Homes story off your mind.' Zadie Smith

A.M. Homes returns with signature humour, compassion and psychological acuity to tell thirteen stories that expose the heart of twenty-first century America.

Available now in hardback and ebook

GRANTA

CHAMELEON

Tomoko Sawada

Introduction by Sayaka Murata

TRANSLATED FROM THE JAPANESE BY GINNY TAPLEY
TAKEMORI

Living as a woman in Japan I have undergone a number of metamorphoses since childhood. Whenever I change my hairstyle, clothes or make-up; my way of talking, tone of voice, or the way I move the muscles in my face, the reaction I get from people around me changes too. At school I started running around in a black T-shirt and brown trousers instead of the pink outfit my mother had chosen for me, and my teacher started treating me like a naughty little tomboy rather than a nice obedient little girl. At university I adopted the flashy so-called *gyaru* (gal) look, bleached my hair brown and wore miniskirts with skin-tight camisoles, looking like one of Sawada's images. I soon found that the progressive girls started inviting me along to offbeat places, bars and clubs; guys asked me out on dates, and I was often chatted up on the street. When I had to get a job I dyed my hair black again and wore natural make-up. The company brass interviewing me commented fondly on what a 'serious girl' I was, and girls dressed exactly like me would strike up conversations. I always tried to metamorphose into my optimal self to fit whatever the context demanded.

As far as I was concerned, clothes and make-up were cosplay tools – simply by changing them I could metamorphose into another character, as if by magic. And then the way other people behaved towards me changed, as though I were a totally different person.

Looking at Sawada's photos now, I am overwhelmed by the feeling that all my transformations, which I always took for granted as something I just did, were actually more peculiar and intriguing than I imagined. I thought of my metamorphoses as a way of emphasising or externalising certain aspects of myself. I assumed that it had to be something that was already there within me, otherwise I would immediately be exposed as a fraud. But if Sawada can transform herself without limit, maybe I can too. Perhaps there is no end to the metamorphoses.

I sometimes find myself judging someone's character after just one glance at their clothes and hairstyle, or their make-up and facial expressions. I used to think that my own gaze as I did so was dishonest. But Sawada's photographs made me realize that this type of human behaviour is rather endearing after all; my imagination runs wild with what Sawada's fabricated personas might be like, how their daily routines go, and what their speech mannerisms might be. I might like some of her characters, and be taken aback by others. I might turn down that one if she turned up for a job interview, while the one next to her looks like a hard worker . . . The way I instantly judge these proliferating Sawadas is frightening, but I also find it rather peculiar and endearing.

Judging someone by their appearance, I think, is also really animal-like. They spread their wings wide during courtship, or make themselves appear larger. Humans wear colourful clothes, paint their faces or tie their hair up in amazing shapes in the hopes of creating a certain impression. These acts of transformation may have a city-like characteristic, but they are also primitive and innate within us. Aliens surely would find this type of human behaviour peculiar and endearing too. The numerous Sawadas in these photographs made me reflect on the strange nature of humanity. What an interesting animal the human is. ∎

TRANSLATOR'S NOTE: The Japanese language is more tolerant of repetition than English. Sayaka Murata's use of words in this piece was very deliberate, and certain words are repeated: 'metamorphose', 'change', 'transform', 'peculiar', 'endearing'.

The term 'cosplay' refers to the practice of dressing up as favourite characters from movies, manga, games and so forth. Murata's use of it here indicates deliberation, not the imitation of particular characters.

MIAI ♥, 2001

OMIAI ♥, 2001

MIAI ♥, 2001

Costume / FUKEI (policewoman), 2003

stume / TAKUSHI-DORAIVA (taxi driver), 2003

TIARA, 2008

Decoration, 2008

Decoration, 2008

Decoration | Face, 2008

Decoration / Face, 2008

cover, 2002

cover, 2002

over, 2002

MASQUERADE, 2006

18.
internationales
literaturfestival
berlin

05 – 15 09 2018

02 09 Sun	**BERLIN LIEST**	
05 09 Wed	**OPENING:** **IGOR LEVIT** [RUS / D] **EVA MENASSE** [A / D] **BURGHART KLAUSSNER** [D]	
06 09 Thu	**FRIDA NILSSON** [S] **AI WEIWEI** [CHN / D]	
07 09 Fri	**CHARMAINE CRAIG** [USA] **MELBA ESCOBAR DE NOGALES** [CO] **OLIVIER GUEZ** [F]	
08 09 Sat	**MASANDE NTSHANGA** [ZA] **BRUCE PASCOE** [AUS]	
09 09 Sun	**SCOTT ANDERSON** [USA] **MARÍA CECILIA BARBETTA** [RA / D]	
10 09 Mon	**SYDNEY SMITH** [CDN]	
11 09 Tue	**JULI ZEH** [D]	
12 09 Wed	**ZAZA BURCHULADZE** [GE] **PRABDA YOON** [T]	
13 09 Thu	**DAVID GRAEBER** [GB]	
14 09 Fri	**DIDIER ERIBON** [F] **MICHAEL ONDAATJE** [CDN] **BERNHARD SCHLINK** [D]	
15 09 Sat	**JENNIFER EGAN** [USA] **MAJA LUNDE** [N] **NIGEL SLATER** [GB]	

06 – 09 09
POETRY NIGHTS

07 – 09 09
DECOLONIZING WOR(L)DS

09 09
GRAPHIC NOVEL DAY

ART OF COOKING
THE EVOLUTION OF HUMAN
CULTURE
NATURE WRITING
POLITICS OF DRUGS
REFUGEES WORLDWIDE

www.literaturfestival.com

TaraShea Nesbit age fourteen, 1995
Courtesy of the author

SEE WHAT YOU DO TO ME

TaraShea Nesbit

'The victim who is able to articulate the situation of the victim has ceased to be a victim: he, or she, has become a threat.' – James Baldwin

She had buck teeth but a lithe body, smooth skin, and I know, from the one glorious time she took her bra off in front of me, breasts as upright and curved as two new bowls. Never did I want to touch something more. She was fourteen and I was twelve. Her hair was the color of a field mouse, cut at her shoulders, shiny and straight, and flipped up naturally at the ends. We lived in the Beaver Ridge Run apartment complex, in a lower-middle-class suburb built in the sixties, before the General Motors plant closed, before the National Cash Register Corporation left.

Sara and I both had younger siblings to watch while our parents worked, both of us responsible daughters. Her parents worked at the factories near our town: a tin factory, a paint factory, then a cannery. Always working and away, it seemed, except on Friday evenings, when they had a large dinner with all the children and a family friend or two. That was the only time I saw her mother, Bernadette, smile, at Richard, her friend, who teased Sara's youngest sibling, still in diapers, and swooped him in his arms. Richard was thirty-six and worked at a barbershop in town. His wife was only twenty-one, and together they had two daughters, three-year-old twins. When I met them, they were both wearing immaculate white sundresses. Richard winked to the children, who loved him, or at least loved the attention. He had found himself a perfect family.

My own mother worked twelve-hour shifts as a respiratory therapist in the neonatal intensive-care unit. She was newly divorced from my stepfather. My father lived on the other side of town, a beauty salesman with a budding clandestine side business of which I knew very little, except that he worked nights. Family friends were not part of our meals.

When we were not at the park with our siblings, we were at Sara's house, with its menagerie of animals and children, which gave the house its particular smell of cat, gerbil and toddler shit. On Sunday mornings Sara would put two quarters in the newspaper dispenser at the 7-Eleven and take all the papers but one, to change the gerbil's cages.

Why leave one? I asked.

So it doesn't look suspicious.

No one ever needed to remind her to do anything, such as chores around the house. She mothered while her mother worked. Both of our mothers would be grandmothers by forty.

We played all day during the winter break and weekends and summer, and then we went straight home and called. In our nearly identical homes – same Formica, same dull carpet, same beige walls – I could imagine her, phone cord looping from the bar in the kitchen and back to the bedroom she shared with her sister. I took the phone to my bedroom and we spoke the inconsequential conversation of girls until one of our mothers called for us to get off the phone. *Someone important could be trying to call,* they would say. We only pushed the limits when we were certain we would not be caught. We were good, responsible daughters. Until that year.

R ichard asked Sara to babysit his twin daughters. After she put the girls to bed, Sara always called me.

But one night, she didn't.

What happened? I asked the next day, as we walked our siblings to the park, shouting their names, telling them to stop at the end of the sidewalk.

When he dropped me off . . .

Richard returned her to the apartment complex, but he parked a block away. He cut the lights. He talked to her, told her how much he cared for her. He took her hand. He kissed it. He asked her if she liked it. She smiled. Then he kissed her on the lips. She was fourteen years old.

I listened to her confession, to what kissing felt like, how he could dream in color, how he could make his dreams go where he wanted them to. How she promised she would not tell anyone about them. He'd been in jail in Kentucky, Sara told me, but she did not know why, or didn't want to tell me. He had been married before.

Sara walked with the lightness of a girl in love.

He's married, I said.

But she opposed me so adamantly – as if I did not understand love, as if I were a child – that I knew if I continued criticizing him I would lose her.

We love one another, she said, and I sort of believed her.

W ith each week's progress, Sara moved further away from me. As Richard inched into Sara's life and body I shrunk to the size of the sixth-grader I was.

At the beginning of the summer, Sara's parents moved out of the apartment complex and into a vinyl-sided house on the corner of the main street leading into east Dayton. The streets were narrow and potholed. The schools were ranked low.

I asked to visit her. Both of my parents, separately, said no. It was the only decision I recall that they had agreed on since their separation ten years prior.

I finished elementary school with an honor-roll ribbon and a yearbook with multiple entries of 'Keep smiling' or 'Smile more'. In the fall I would begin seventh grade, choosing between two junior high schools: the junior high on the wealthier west side of town, or the middle school, where parents worked the assembly lines, maintenance and food service.

I kept asking to visit Sara in Dayton. After many nos and much complaining on my part, my parents finally let me go. My mother dropped me off. I wore cut-off jeans and a T-shirt as Sara and I walked the neighborhood. I wasn't wearing anything revealing, but trucks honked at us, men whistled from their porches, and at the post office, men turned in line to look us up and down. The attention was striking. Men stared directly, gawked.

Where were Sara's parents? Gone. Who knows. *It is violent here,* I thought, hearing the car alarms, imagining all the robberies that must be taking place, not realizing how easy it was for an alarm to be triggered.

In the street, wondering which car got robbed, I met a neighbor boy, Jason. He was sweet, but I took my cues about how to talk to members of the opposite sex from what was around me: my mother's self-help books, like *Men Are From Mars, Women Are From Venus,* and the men on the morning talk show on Z-93, who paid a woman five hundred dollars to drive to work topless. I saw a picture of her later in the news from the shoulders up.

I asked Jason about the size of his dick. I had never asked anyone this before, but I was in a new city, and trying out boldness.

But how many inches is it?

He demurred.

Go measure.

He demurred. I pressed, I pressed.

His mother's calls for him grew louder and more urgent.

I really have to go, he said.

Back inside, he called me on the phone.

Soft or hard? he whispered.

I didn't know what he meant so I covered the receiver and said to Sara, *He said, 'Soft or hard?'*

Sara just shook her head.

That night at her house, we slept in her twin-sized bed, but I did not sleep. I do not think we spoke of Richard, not because they were no longer involved, but rather because they were so involved that her alliances had shifted. She was keeping the secret she initially promised she would keep.

I had not been kissed or touched, with one exception. My stepfather had a swastika tattoo on his right arm and a nose broken so many times that it swooped to the right side when looked at straight on. He used his belt on my toddler brothers' backsides, and once broke the skin until it bled. When I was nine I kissed him goodbye and slipped my tongue into his mouth like I had seen my mom do. He stiffened, pulled back, and said, *We don't do that, Sissy. This can be our special kiss,* and instead rubbed my nose to his. He nearly drowned my mother once in a river in Kentucky, but he did not want my tongue in his mouth. Sometimes what men did not do was more startling than what they did. When my mother found out she said, *Who taught you that? Who? Tell me,* the way a mother does when she herself has been molested. But what my mother could not keep me from was my own stubborn wish to have something for myself, my curiosity for knowledge in all forms, for taking whatever was offered.

I turned thirteen in late July. My mother got call waiting. Sara and I spoke less and less frequently. I turned to other friends from the complex, swam at the pool, watched television. But when my mother worked I was not allowed to leave the house, though my brothers, diagnosed as hyperactive, could play outside. My mother was terrified something would happen to me, an unchaperoned girl wearing her first bra.

One afternoon while my brothers were outside and my mother was still at work, I reached Sara on the phone.

What are you doing? I asked.

Douching.

She said it like a secret.

What is that? And why?

I'm babysitting tonight.

She said Richard had a plan to leave Joy out and come back home early. I told her it was unsafe to use her mother's douche. *You could get an infection.* I did not have actual knowledge of this as a fact, it just seemed like it could be true and something in her voice scared me.

In her silence, I saw a shrug, and began to worry about Sara.

A few weeks later, Sara was babysitting again. She asked me to call at 8.30 p.m. But this time, Richard answered the phone.

I hung up.

Then my own phone rang.

Hello? I said, scared and thrilled.

Who is this? Richard asked. His voice so deep.

I paused. He asked again. I told him I was Sara's friend.

Is Sara there? I asked.

She is home already. And what are you doing calling my house?

I apologized. I told him sometimes we talked after the girls went to bed.

So when I'm paying her to play with my children she's talking on the phone to you?

I paused and apologized again and said it wasn't like that.

Is anyone at your house? he asked.

Asleep. My mother had to wake at 5 a.m. to have enough time to shower, get the boys ready for day care, drop them off, and drive into Dayton to be at the hospital by the start of her 7 a.m. shift.

So, what do Sara and I do together? he asked me.

Oh, how I knew, how I knew, I thought, everything. And how I had been sworn to complete secrecy.

She's your babysitter? I said.

The uptick in my voice, the question, gave him a chuckle.

Hang on a minute, he said, and I heard a screen door creak open. He was stepping outside. He wanted to talk to me.

He would call me at ten, after everyone had gone to bed. Since we now had call waiting, I called Time and Temperature at 9.59 p.m. and stayed on the phone, listening to the weather and the time, the forecast and the time, again and again until the phone beeped. Then I settled into my bed and talked about my day. I complained about my mother, my nosy brothers, my homework, my friends. Because he was outside my family and not someone who would gossip about me at school I told him everything I hated and longed for. I told him so much, unconscious of how he would use that information: absent mother, absent father, lonely thirteen-year-old girl who can't leave the house because of her mother's fear. I was looking for wisdom. He was assessing how much of a risk I was, how likely I was to tell people what we might do, how easily I could become a victim.

After a few evening calls, our conversations veered into all of the things he would like to do to me. In response to his questions, I lied and said yes, I was touching my body.

One night he asked, *Could you sneak out?*

Yeah, I said, trying on a casual voice.

Meet me next to the building behind yours.

I checked my hair and clothes. There was nothing to be done. I put a stick of gum in my mouth. I climbed on my bed, slid the window open, and walked out into the warm summer air. Crickets, cicadas, the joy of real air, not sterile air conditioning. I turned the corner and there he was, the man I'd been talking to in secret for weeks, reaching over into the passenger side of a beat-up blue Honda, opening the door for me. While my mother was asleep and my father was across town arranging business deals, I was in a Honda Civic kissing a man older than my father.

Richard took my hand. He told me how nice it was to see me, to talk in person. Ten minutes passed this way. He put his lips to mine.

Then he looked over at me with a serious expression and said, *Don't do this with anyone else.*

I laughed.

You could get really hurt. There are bad people out there.

I interpreted this as proof that he was someone who could get jealous, proof that he cared for me. I did not ask him about Sara, but he spoke of her a few times. He felt, I think, a fondness for her that he thought of as love. I hoped she was not still babysitting for him, that she had moved on. When we last spoke she had told me of a new man ten years older than her, who I just had to meet. I did meet him, the one time I skipped school. He took us to the Air Force Museum and fingered her in the stars and planets exhibit. She was kind enough to tell me what fingering was without making it seem like I did not know.

I snuck back into my bedroom. I was freer than before, I thought. I had something that was mine. The luminous idea of a secret.

That night when he got home, he called.

I had such a nice time with you. I hope I dream of you, he said.

I fell asleep replaying the sensations his touches gave me.

A week later, and newly thirteen, I started junior high at the west-side, wealthier school. My mother left the house in the dark and dropped my brothers off at day care.

I told Richard to look out for her red Buick with the MY CHILD IS AN HONOR STUDENT AT BEAVER RIDGE ELEMENTARY SCHOOL bumper sticker on it. I told him where she parked, her assigned parking spot in front of our house. If her car was gone, so was she. I was doing the one thing my mother had tried to warn me about.

Early on a Friday morning, my first week in seventh grade, Richard knocked on my door, so lightly I thought I might have imagined it. I felt a tingling throughout my body.

I opened the door.

He whispered, *Is anyone here?*

He asked if I was sure. He asked with real fear, as if he had been caught before. I registered this as paranoia and laughed.

He stared hard at me.

I answered loudly, *No. Of course not, come in.*

L*ock the door,* he said.
No one is going to come in.

He stared at me.

I locked the door.

He raised his eyebrows at the top lock.

I locked the deadbolt, too.

He was short, eye-level with me. With the doors locked twice, he kissed me. I smelled coffee, the cheap kind that comes in a can.

He kissed my neck, then ran his tongue along it, up to my earlobe, breathing warm air and soft kisses into my ear. I wanted to match his skill, but this was my first real kiss. How should my lips be, my mouth? Where should my hands go? They hung down at my side.

See what you do to me, he said, and moved my right hand down past his belt, to the zipper of his soft Dickies work pants. I felt a hard bump.

See what you do to me, he said again.

There was allure, confusion and fear. *I* was an irresistible temptation.

But I pulled my hand away. He had crow's feet and a weathered face, which made me feel superior.

Do you know what this is? he asked and put my hand back to his cock. *It's how much you excite me.*

He kissed me urgently again and led me toward the couch, then asked, *Where is your bedroom?*

I walked backwards, kissing him, leading him to my bedroom. Gone was the brass daybed my mother bought me one summer when I was six and we lived in Florida. On my last birthday, I got a full-size mattress and box spring on the floor, and on it was my first bedspread. It was reversible – one side was navy, one side was white with navy stripes.

He moved his hands up my shirt and with one motion, unhooked my first bra. He asked, afterwards, if this was okay. I nodded.

He said, *Say it.*

I said, *This is okay.*

We kissed and he cupped my breasts and I touched the outside of his pants until seven fifteen.

At seven fifteen he drove me to school in a rusted ivory pickup. He parked a block away. We must have looked like father and child. Then he drove himself to the barbershop where he worked, three blocks from the school.

He was twenty-four years older than me.

By day, Richard cut hair. In the evening, he drove his rusted truck to a wooden house in south Dayton. In the morning, before work, he came to my apartment.

He told me about his disgust at the women who walked by the barbershop in heels and wearing lipstick on their way to the bagel shop.

What's wrong with heels? I asked.

That clackety-clack-clack, he said. In winter it was not practical. I did not like it when he spoke of adult women this way, even though I liked that he didn't admire them. But what would he think of me when I had grown up?

I changed the subject and asked what his favorite music was.

Traditional country, he said, like Lee Greenwood, so I ordered Lee Greenwood's greatest hits from the BMG Music Club.

On his second visit, he put his finger in my vagina. I held my breath and stiffened, preparing for more pain.

Is this okay? he said, and put my hand on his cock. *See what you do to me.*

It was a molehill, but I was doing something to him, so I focused there instead, on my ability to create excitement in him rather than the monotonous in and out of his finger.

You are so tight, he said, and I apologized.

He smiled and kissed me more urgently.

We heard a sound from the apartment upstairs. He stopped, shifted, looked toward the door.

What was that? he asked.

I told him it was the neighbor. I told him to relax. I reminded him it was a garden-level apartment, easy to climb out of if my mother came home.

Had someone else invited me to sneak out of my house and meet them, had they been vetted by a friend, as Sara had vetted Richard, I would have met them, too. I had a boyfriend now, a sweet boy who was in eighth grade, nicknamed Oregano Joe because he once tried to sell oregano as marijuana. I spoke to him on the phone briefly most evenings, but inwardly I groaned each time he called – how unwise and infantile peer conversations seemed. Twice we had gone to the movies. His affable stepfather picked me up in a conversion van with airbrushed beach scenes on the side panels, and drove us, as we held hands secretly in the back seat, to the Dollar Movie Theater. I mentioned the boyfriend to Richard, hoping he would be jealous. He said it was good for me to be with boys my age, which made me feel like a baby.

When, on the next visit, Richard slipped a second finger into my vagina I thought, *I do not like this.* I thought, *This is what he did with her*, and felt closer to my friend, Sara, in one way, and then further away from her than ever.

The clitoris was a discovery I had already made. Richard moved one finger, and then two, in and out of my vagina as if his fingers were a toilet brush. In the background, Lee Greenwood sang how proud he was to be American.

Richard would have been a better pedophile had he known how to warm a female body up.

And yet, I was lured by my desire for knowledge. What were the bounds of physical sensation? What could another person do to me? I had a school boyfriend, but I knew that I could not explore these things with a school boyfriend. A school boyfriend would tell people. Going beyond kissing with a school boyfriend would get you labeled a slut.

One morning when Richard was over, the phone rang. We were in my bedroom. Richard made for the window.

Just wait, I said, coolly.

Hello?

What's wrong with you? my mother said.

Nothing, I said, trying to readjust my voice.

Richard moved in to me and kissed my neck. So close to my mother's voice. I pushed him away.

She reminded me to unload the dishwasher and turn down the Crockpot before I left for school.

I said okay. She was my mother then. Perhaps sensing something was off, that afternoon she surprised me by coming home early. I was drinking hot chocolate and doing homework when she came in with my brothers.

On his next visit, he led me back to my bedroom and lay me down on the striped side of my reversible bedspread. We kissed until the sun made a harsh morning light that showed his wrinkles and his buck teeth. Richard pulled down his pants. He pulled down his white underwear. I saw his scarred, crooked, thick penis, the first one I had ever seen. He pulled the skin back to appear larger, but came across instead as insecure.

Look what you do to me.

I smiled. This was supposed to be empowerment. But empowerment was telling him no again and again, empowerment – as I thought of it then, though I did not know the word – was the books I read and the movies I watched: Maya Angelou's 'Phenomenal Woman' read by Janet Jackson in *Poetic Justice*. Empowerment was a man looking at you – every curve – and you declining.

He approached my face with his cock.

I turned my head away.

Let me lay it next to you, he said.

He put his upright cock against my cotton panties, the tip lying on my stomach, and looked at me as if I would not be able to resist this alluring thing so close to my body.

He asked me to take off my panties.

I just want to lay it next to you, he said.

I squeaked out a no.

Instead, he slid his cock through the leg hole of my panties. I could feel it up my leg and between the lips of my vagina. Our bodies were constricted by my underwear. He moved in a bobbing motion, the shaft of his penis rubbing against my skin.

He leaned in and kissed me with his stubbly face. His body held no allure. The only desire he offered was being desired.

He slid his cock out of my panties and climbed off me, his pants around his ankles. He got on his knees and pulled me to him. My bra was askance. One breast flopped out and the other was beneath the thinly padded lace and polyester.

Just kiss it, he said, and moved my shoulders downward.

I turned my mouth away.

No, thank you, I said, as if he were a friend's grandmother offering candies.

Don't you want to? he said. And then that refrain, *See what you do to me?*

Yes, I thought, this attracts you. Now tease me to the point of extreme anticipation, give my body warmth and tingling, show me what it feels like with another person. But he never did.

Come here, he said.

When I did, he pushed my head downward.

Try it, he said, the most forceful he had been. He shoved my mouth onto his cock.

His cock was in my mouth and because of his force, I gagged. I lifted my head up.

He apologized, but with happiness.

I sat away from him and fixed my bra.

Have you had your period yet?

I had, two years prior, at Sara's house. She had shown me how to insert a tampon. I confirmed I had started my period, but left out the other details.

He frowned. Then he sighed.

We should get you to school, he said.

That was the last time I saw Richard in my mother's apartment. We both knew this was not leading anywhere. I took another look at that surgically wrecked penis, calculated how unwet he made my body, and knew that I would never consent to *Just kiss it* or *Let me lay it next to you.* None of it was interesting beyond what I had gleaned in those few months of heavy petting. He stopped calling. So did I.

Why didn't I tell anyone? And why did I pursue my best friend's pedophile? The lure of knowledge was greater than loyalty. I did not feel powerless, but powerful. It was I who was desired. I did not speak because I did not want to see the disappointment on my parents' faces. Richard told me he could read people's thoughts and visit their dreams. He told me this, obviously, to try to contain me, to ensure our secret was not out. I let him believe that I believed him.

But I tested him. *Oh yeah? What am I thinking right now?* I said. He said something about fear and excitement and that I desired him.

Nope, I said.

What then?

I was thinking about an elephant.

I *was* thinking about an elephant – I already knew it as a thing one can't *not* imagine when asked to.

But he just said, *Huh?*

He never said he loved me. Confessing love would be the strongest tool for girls like us. I hoped for it, not because I loved him, but because I always wanted the ultimate.

A year later Richard and Sara were distant childhood memories. But then Sara called my father's house, where I'd been staying.

For you, my father said. I picked up my bedroom phone.

How could you? she said.

I said nothing.

Why did you do it? she asked. *Why did you?*

In her voice was rage and betrayal, but not disbelief. She saw my disloyalty – to my social class, to my neighborhood, to my family, to my friends. The disloyalty that would later enable me to separate emotionally from them, leave them, leave Ohio.

I did not speak. She hung up.

When I called her back to apologize, her younger sister answered. She said Sara was not there. *She says never call her again.*

Soon after, my father suspected I was getting into trouble, so he read my diary. In it, I had written down everything I had done with Richard. He called the police. They photocopied every page and called me in.

A white man of about forty-five asked the questions. *What did you do with Richard?*

We sat on a bench, I said.

Where? he asked.

The park. The park by my house.

What did you do together? he asked again.

Talked.

He gave me a skeptical look.

Had he been a woman, I might have said more. A woman would have seen through me.

I saw I would have to confess something, to give him something. But I'd watched detective shows. I knew it was quite possible that my father was behind those mirrored walls. I thought of him, his disappointment and his belief in my ability to, as he said, *achieve anything you want.* How he wanted me to finish college, as he had not. How he wanted me to make money, legally. I thought of how I had disappointed him in wanting something so lascivious, so base, so vile, with someone so ordinary, or, rather, so perverse.

We kissed, I said to the investigator.

You kissed?

Yes.

How often?

Once.

Once? he said, eyebrows arched.

Once. I repeated and repeated, *We sat on a bench and kissed once.*

What else?

Nothing.

This went on for several minutes.

When I started to cry, he pressed me more. I stuck to my story.

He stepped out of the room, came back and said, *Okay. You can go.*

I was protecting Richard, saving him from jail time, but that was not my intention. My intention was to protect myself, and not to have to go back on my word. If I told a lie, I stuck to it. I thought it was the only way.

For months, my father called the police again and again to check the status of the case. I listened in on the other phone. The detective said, *She says it was a single kiss. I can't make a case on that.*

A nother year went by. I was nearing the end of high school. I got a job at Discovery Zone, an indoor playground at the mall, as a birthday-party hostess. When there weren't birthdays, I ran concession. One quiet Wednesday afternoon they came in. Richard ordered pizza and soda from another person working concession. Sara held the hands of his two children. I did not look at her directly. I had a Discovery Zone baseball cap on, and imagined that from this 'disguise' she would not recognize me. *Should I say hello?* I wondered. I felt dread, and the recognition of what I had done came back as shame. We acted like we did not know one another. Did I think she would not remember me? I wondered if she was pregnant. To speak to her would be to acknowledge what I had done, when all I wanted was for the action to go away. I hid in the kitchen, dunking dirty plates into the sink. I hid until it was time to host another party, and when I emerged, Sara, Richard and the two daughters were gone.

R ecently, I took a job at a university an hour from the apartment complex I grew up in. Now that I am a mother and teacher, working with young women from the neighborhoods I know from childhood, Richard's story is acutely on my mind. How many threats are out there for my daughter and for my students? I visit the Ohio legislature website to learn the statute of limitations. Could I help stop one pedophile? The Ohio Special Statute of Limitations for Childhood Sexual Abuse, effective 3 August 2006, limits victims' ability to report and prosecute a perpetrator to twelve years. I am thirty-six. Richard entered my mother's apartment twenty-three years ago. It took me twenty-three years to understand I was not fully culpable for opening the door to my mother's house, and see beyond myself to what a threat he posed to others. When the Ohio Statute ran out, I was in Denver, getting a PhD, writing stories, biking across town with my new husband and friends, mourning aspects of my family and relationships, but not thinking about Richard. All that time, he was in Ohio, raising daughters. Did Richard note the years and breathe more easily? Or was there always a twelve-year clock, always a girl or two? Is there now?

My husband and I read picture books to our three-year-old daughter about winter approaching. In one, the female narrator says that the rabbits in the forest are alert because danger is out there everywhere.

What is danger? our daughter asks.

We fumble to find the words to describe this to her without scaring her so much that she will not sleep through the night.

Recently, before she began preschool, I talked to her of consent. I told her that her body is hers alone, that nobody can touch it unless she says so. But it is difficult to do this and not evoke too much fear.

Why do people need to ask? she said.

So far, the only way I've seen consent materialize is that now if I kiss my daughter's forehead she says, with a mischievous smile and a low voice, *You have to ask.* Then she puts her lips on mine. When I return the kiss she smiles and says again, *Mommy, you have to ask.* ∎

© JONGSUK YOON
Insomnia, 2015
Courtesy of Galerie nächst St Stephan Rosemarie Schwarzwälder

ON THE TROUBLE OF BOUND ASSOCIATION

Lisa Wells

I'd gone to see the Italian psychoanalyst in the hopes she'd help me navigate a personal crisis. But as you probably already know, and I came to understand, psychoanalysis tends not to be the best methodology for negotiating the acute, unless by acute you mean the lifespan. In this case, I'd allotted an hour.

I'll come to the crisis in a moment, but first let me say, this analyst was an impressive woman in several senses. There was the visual: she wore glossy leather boots and poufy slacks pegged tightly at the ankles, and a cherry-red blazer with immense shoulder pads. I'd guess she was in her mid-to-late sixties. Her dyed blond hair was undercut and side-swept in a severe new-wave bang that obscured half her face. The visible half toggled between expressions of amusement, consternation and narcotic fatigue (its resting state). But the most striking thing about this woman was to be heard, not seen. She spent the entire session talking *at* me, in heavily accented English that began in my ear as noise, and slowly clarified over the hour, as if the stereocilia of my cochlea had been individually attuned. My presence in the room was required, but my *self* was incidental – a familiar feeling. I spoke twice, and briefly. Lodged in the cleft of the leather couch, sweating, I spoke from my neck, as if choked. Her stream of free association was otherwise unbroken, a stream that spidered out and seemed to touch, at once, the most intimate truths of individual existence, the family, and the whole geopolitical saga of human history.

This did not take place in Italy, by the way. Her office was located in a sort of adobe strip mall, in the improbable locale of Tucson, Arizona, where I lived at the time, uneasily. As she spoke, my attention wound its way to the incongruity of the scene and raised a couple of questions: *What is this fabulously butch Janus – apparently excised from a Patrick Nagel print – doing in Tucson, Arizona? And why on Earth would she stay here?* As fate would have it, my aforementioned difficulty was related to the latter question.

Had I the extra income to pay this fascinating woman to talk at me each week, I might have gone back. My exposure to older women was limited in that desert, and when I did encounter an admired older woman (writers, for the most part), 90 per cent of the time their orientation toward me seemed rivalrous or dismissive. Then again, I was a chronic ingratiator, a real suck-up, and they may have been repulsed by my female conditioning; perhaps it raised the specter of a former self? In any case, a fair share of the misogyny I'd weathered in my life had been at the bequest of other women, which confused, for me, the whole sisterhood solidarity thing. In fact, this confusion, particularly as it pertained to the *ur-woman* (my mother), was another reason I'd sought analytical counsel.

But my most pressing concern that afternoon was an increased sense of estrangement from human beings of all genders. People frequently talked *at* me, just as this analyst had, with seemingly little regard for my interiority. I no longer knew how to make myself known to the other, and I was hoping to narrate some of my tenuous inner life aloud before it evaporated for good. *I need a blanker screen,* I told myself then. Now I'm inclined to think she was exactly who I was looking for.

Were I my own analyst, reading this text, I might notice how strenuously I avoid the topic at hand, the movement known as #MeToo, by focusing on another woman. I avoid the topic at hand because it overwhelms me, has come to touch – like that loquacious analyst's riff – not only my personal ledger of slights, but the whole of human experience: from the workplace to the bedroom, the family, the grocery checkout line, the various national and cultural histories of our respective subjugations and the many ways we are complicit in keeping one another silent and in line. I was cresting a mute wave of materia prima, and somewhere down in my id I sensed it was soon to break, or I was.

At 4.30 a.m. I wake in the grip of what my husband has dubbed 'the roving perseverator'. At 4.30, I am concerned about the steepness of the stairs leading to our bedroom. I slipped and fell down them the other day, banged up my shoulder and somehow sprained my big toe, and soon we'll have subletters living in the house. The subletters are in their seventies and I imagine the slip, the fracture, the anesthesiologist, the sleep they won't wake up from, the lawsuit, life's remainder tormented by guilt. I resolve to order two boxes of transparent grip tape for the stairs, but now I'm worried about the height of the banister. Were we to remedy the banister, my mind might alight on the low clearance of the basement ceiling. This is why the perseverator is 'roving'. There is always a fatality to anticipate, there is always a warning to be issued, an intervention to be made. Lapsed vigilance virtually secures disaster. The rover never rests.

And so my mind has felt its way in the dark to the subject of my mother. 5.15 a.m. My mother has high blood pressure, and I've asked her to do a difficult thing. I've asked her to join me in confronting the family member who, once upon a time, molested me. Current atmospheric pressures have made this secret difficult to ignore. The family is tightly knit, and should the confrontation take place, it could unstitch our social fabric in a swift instant. Or not. I don't know.

I think I've made my peace with the possibilities, but I know they've caused my mother considerable grief in recent days, and not a little insomnia. I also know – or have vaguely been made to understand – that some of what she's wrestling with is her own history: undisclosed traumas I've only guessed at, that have rendered her chronically anxious and somewhat remote. I'm concerned about her blood pressure. I'm worried she'll keel over from the stress of my request. I'm worried her sleeplessness will cause her to drive recklessly and crash. I am powerful enough to kill or save whomever I think about.

Like my mother, I love the man who hurt me. I am similar to my mother, and resent her for this, and love her desperately, and would do anything to spare her the pain I know is coming. Even if, perhaps especially if, it ensures my own. That's how it was transmitted, what little I know about being a woman.

Vigilance, dissociation, repressed anger, codependence, the redundant negative fantasy – these are the symptoms of what I circle. Can I differentiate this psychic activity from the supposed bedrock of my character? To put it another way: how am I not my symptoms?

So why bring up the analyst? Somewhere in that beguiling torrent of speech, in listing the various forces of nature and nurture that shape our lives, she said – and she stressed this – that the one force we cannot completely know is the zeitgeist. We cannot know our era as it's unfolding. Its developments are at once diffuse and acute, the web of interactions it spins are beyond the total comprehension of any individual. Only time affords distance enough to grasp the whole gestalt, and as any student of history knows, even those more distant descriptions are perspectival and up for debate.

Meanwhile, you wake, feed yourself, deal with the bills; the days stack up, obscuring youth's immortal visions. These days, every day plagued by the hashtag. Every day, facing it. Hearing the testimonies, crying on the treadmill, riding the wave of associations, battling the inner patriarch, revisiting the violations, the ways I've been complicit, circumscribed, afraid – then I turn away. My mind has flipped as often as it's been engaged and now I'm tired. Much as I am wary of any politics arriving in 140 characters, it turns out this trending cultural shorthand applies to me too.

Still, I thought: *I have nothing to say.* It's too soon, the zeitgeist is still unfolding, it's too confusing, and too fraught a terrain to unpack with candor. Then I thought: surely I'm not the only one inwardly choked by this cultural moment. Surely, when considering the effects of a system that ventriloquizes us all to varied extents, a system that is at once global and personal, historic and contemporary, a system of abuse in which offenders are also loved ones – I can't be the only one feeling confused.

I found a blanker screen. Doctor C., the trauma magician, the sort that waggles her fingers before your eyes and rarely speaks. The endeavor of Eye Movement Desensitization and Reprocessing, or EMDR, depends on the ability to time travel. Some people can't bear to remain inside the vessel. I can do it, but not easily. The process is this: you go back in time to the most hideous shit of your life, and sit in that shit while the doctor 'bilaterally stimulates' your brain. As I understand it – and this is a plebeian's take – unresolved trauma harbors in the brain's right hemisphere, in implicit memory, until 'triggered', at which point it blooms through the body, engaging the nervous system in present tense. This is what's sometimes called a 'flashback'. It's believed that if you track the doctor's fingers with your eyes, you can sort of drag the memory into the left hemisphere, where it becomes explicit, and a story can be made. The story, like most stories, locates the phenomena in time (the desired tense, in this case, is *past*), and in arranging its chaos into a linear coherence, the storyteller is desensitized to the memory.

Storytelling – more precisely, *telling one's story in community* – is one of the stages of trauma recovery, as articulated by Judith Herman in her foundational study of PTSD. But the ability to move the story out into the environment depends on earlier stages, namely, developing capacity for managing distressing sensations, and establishing safety within one's body and relationships. (Of course, this raises questions about what qualifies as safety within the broader context of, say, a 'rape culture'.) The restorative technology of telling one's story in community is an old one, but opportunities can be scarce these days – at least in the secular US, where I live. Peer recovery meetings can provide the context, as can restorative justice circles and, I suppose, social-media platforms. Considering that trauma resides in and is reprocessed through the body, I'm skeptical that any disembodied exchange can serve as a substitute for people in a room together, though it may inspire one to seek that room.

I'd gone to the analyst's office believing it was my turn to talk. Instead, I was asked to listen. When finally I was able to hear her, I learned a valuable lesson about the limits of my own comprehension. These days, I sometimes feel I'm being talked at by a hundred thousand voices, and the cacophony can overwhelm. Overwhelmed, I might grow rigid and defensive, I might want to lash out (see: *backlash*). But when I stop and tune in to any individual voice, I notice, most of the time, it is simply telling a story. Whether or not I listen, and whether or not I learn something from what I hear, is my decision.

The flashback is an expedient form of time travel. You're twenty-two years old, in the backpackers' hostel, hot and heavy with the Israeli boy. He rasps softly in your ear, *I want to rape you*. Now you are also seven and eight years old, leaping from the bed, wielding the little desk chair, prepared to smash his beautiful skull. Or you're nineteen, napping one summer afternoon with your boyfriend. You wake with a start to his finger in your vagina. This might be a rude awakening for a lot of people, but in your case it is especially jarring as it mirrors the first violation.

They're both mortified. They both cry. You observe this display from the planet of dissociation (they always cry; you never can). It was just a bad translation. He'd meant to say something like 'I want to ravish you', cheap romance-novel stuff, but no nefarious intent. Or you'd been responsive in your sleep, indicating consciousness; a kind of game where you moan and pretend to sleep while he *ravishes you*. Both men cross a line, but you don't presume those crossings would affect all women in the same way, or necessarily at all. The negative effects are amplified by your particular history. A lot is lost in translation. In the body's instantaneous translation of a perceived threat to the cascade of incoherent sensation – terror you don't have the capacity to name, let alone address.

Many relationships are lost this way. In the freezing or lashing out. In the flight from self, in the reflexive assumption of the more distant *you*.

On the one hand, you are tempted to say *we should acknowledge the complications with humility*. On the other, *humility* hasn't seemed to serve 'us' all that well thus far.

Immediately following my second visit to Doctor C., I have a dream. My mother and I are in a dark warehouse, standing before the open door of a refrigerator, our faces bathed in its extraterrestrial light. There's an altercation, and we lock arms in a sort of tango. Our struggle is a dance, but it's also a mirror. However I move, she moves in perfect sync. I look into her face, flashing with alternating waves of terror and rage, and understand that her face is also my face. I lean into that face I love, close enough to kiss it, and scream *YOUR ANGER IS KILLING ME.*

The child concerns herself with the mother's body; the body that is at once the purveyor of exile and her only home. She studies the peace of the body, its health and desires, its availability, its integrity. She senses the residue of violation, its boundaries and psychic perforations. She senses her own power, in the violence of having been born, to reconstitute the mother's former torments. She longs to apply her own body as poultice to the wound. She thinks magically, 'I'll wear your wound for you.' Even now – thirty-five years estranged, old enough to know better – the child believes there's a way back home.

Of the family's fraught magnetism, James Agee wrote: 'and none can care, beyond that room; and none can be cared for, by any beyond that room: and it is small wonder they are drawn together so cowardly close . . . and wonder only that an age that has borne its children and must lose and has lost them, and lost life, can bear further living; but so it is.'

So it is, we survive, and lose each other. And losing each other is one of the ways we have learned to survive. The estrangement from self and other passes down through the generations; passed in the striking hand, the inappropriate touch, the hand that dismisses, the hand that does not lift to intervene. But maybe it doesn't have to be this way.

As Doctor C. instructed: *You can't change what happened, but you can decide it stops with you.*

How does it stop with me, exactly? I don't know for certain, but I do understand a few things. It's my understanding that human beings are social creatures, that much of our cultural conditioning is expressed subconsciously, automatically, and will likely continue to be enacted as such until an interrogation is staged. It's my understanding that the project of eradicating 'weakness' in boys through violence and humiliation is one mechanism by which victims become violators. (It's an analytic axiom: we seek to control or destroy in others what we have disavowed in ourselves.) I understand that the staging of this *interrogation* depends on much: on access to theory and testimony, on subcultural alliances, on socioeconomic status, on intellectual ability, on the victim-turned-perpetrator circuit, on access to help in breaking the circuit – the list goes on.

The call-out can serve to accelerate things. There may, in fact, be no more effective way to incite the necessary transformation. But I also understand that exclusion breeds despair, hostility, is experienced in the body as physical pain, and I wonder what will become of those we've denounced and banished. I wonder where those energies will accumulate, and how they will reconstitute down the line – how they're showing up even now. I wonder, on one hand, if this moment could be leveraged to heal our estrangements, rather than multiply them. On the other hand, the healing of men isn't up to me.

In any case, it seems this trauma is shared, though we bear its effects unequally; a trauma that deadens us to our own experience and to one another. A deadening that helps to facilitate, in turn, the killing of the world, in which all but a few of us are complicit.

These seem to me to be the stakes. But I can't say for sure. The zeitgeist is still unfolding.

During my fourth session with Doctor C. a kind of miracle happened. I'd traveled back in time to the night the man broke into my sleep, and I suddenly remembered the nightgown I'd been wearing: a knee-length baseball T with three-quarter sleeves and a pixelated image of a forest down the front. I hadn't thought of that nightgown in twenty-five years, but all at once I could access dozens of other occasions when I'd worn it. These too were implicit memories – pure embodied emotion – cut long ago from the story I'd made of my family, returned to my body in present tense: dancing with my older sister, pulling an orange from my stocking Christmas morning, curled in my mother's lap as she stroked my hair. It all came back. My sister, my mother – they came back to me. The body remembers what the child cannot bear to know, but suppressing the pain takes the joy away with it. And this is part of what we stand to gain, all of us, from the reckoning. I mean to say, though it's dark inside the shadow and the passage is uncertain, there is gold there, too. Gold enough to guide us through, home to one another. ∎

© DANIEL KUKLA
Lost Horse, 2012
from the *Edge Effect* series

WILD FAILURE

Zoe Whittall

They're driving their failing relationship into the desert. Jasper pulls the car onto the edge of the thinning highway and gets out to take photos. Teprine presses a palm against the rental car window, comparing her skin to the burning hues beyond. She props her phone up, clicks a lazy burst of landscape shots. She will love the memory of having been here.

She doesn't understand how to travel. All she sees is endless metaphor. Humans are small, the Earth is infinite and murderous. *If I get out of the car, I will fall off the planet.* The seat belt cleaves her chest. She appreciates the way it holds her down. Her skin isn't enough. Contained, she sucks on a mango Popsicle from the last gas station, her fingers smelling like sanitizer, applied hourly.

There's a tenderness to the desert's red landscape. She's never seen a desert before.

Teprine re-met Jasper at the supermarket the day after she turned thirty-nine. They knew each other from around the community – that queer small town nestled in the mouth of every sprawling city. She was wearing sweatpants with a coleslaw stain splattered across both knees. It looked like cum and she didn't care. She'd tried to hide when she looked up from the Concord grapes and saw him smelling a tomato. She'd counted out four minutes in the bakery, but still ended up behind him in the checkout.

'Hey, how's it going?' She hadn't spoken out loud in two days and could barely manage this strained greeting.

'I'm getting divorced,' he'd said.

She'd blushed, embarrassed. 'Me too.'

He was remarkably handsome, even under the anaemic lights of Fiesta Farms. She'd never have asked him out, but the divorce had made her emotionally reckless. Also, she was more afraid of the open sky than social rejection.

Holding their green plastic grocery bags, she was a recovered agoraphobic in danger of a relapse, clinging to tight walls, familiar bus routes, the comfort of crowds. He was a trans man who felt most free away from human scrutiny, at peace while hiking off into the distance. After two shy dates, they kissed in a way that anaesthetized the heartbreak. Alone, they were floating heads. Together they reminded each other that a body is capable of imprudent elation.

In motion, Teprine can keep things in perspective. The car is a mobile piece of the familiar. The familiar is a mental salve. Whenever the car stops, her heart runs up into her throat. Her thoughts blur and blend. She was raised in a valley, her bedroom window opened onto upward meadows. She felt safe in the warm embrace of their farmhouse, anchored by packed snow.

She licks the Popsicle stick clean. The thrum of her spatial anxiety sounds like an amplifier on its last legs. When the outside gets too overwhelming, she pictures curling up under the drive shaft like a cat. She touches the window barrier between her vacated body and the edge of Joshua Tree National Park. She can see that it is beautiful. Of course. But it's like looking at a pastoral oil painting she doesn't feel anything for. It could have been a greasy portrait in a hotel room. She can see him in the rear-view mirror taking endless photos. They haven't passed another vehicle in almost an hour.

He gets back in the car. She bites into the Popsicle stick. The rush of air conditioning tucks her hair behind her ears. Soothing. She makes her face into an expression that approximates relaxed and easy-going. Her mouth says, *I can be a fun girl!*

He smiles at her and squeezes her leg. He pulls out a paper map, runs his finger along a line so thin it looks like an accidental pencil scrawl. 'This old road is supposed to be amazing,' he says. 'Should we take it?'

He is so excited to veer off course. She doesn't want to say no, but immediately imagines the car breaking down, and no one finding their bodies for days. They have only a small bottle of coconut water in a fabric bag in the back seat and a cold brew coffee between her thighs. She doesn't want to disappoint him, but she hears herself say, 'Let's take the regular highway, it's going to get dark.'

He pulls away, a half-frown.

Later, in the hotel, Teprine will lie awake as he snores gently and feel a shame so acute that she will long to be stranded on an old road waiting for the sun to kill them.

They'd been planning the trip for months. Jasper would attend a conference in Arizona while she'd work on a manuscript, and then they'd drive to California for a vacation. She'd taken a book out of the library about women who travel to far-flung places by themselves. They talked about being transformed. She wanted that. She was sick of her face in the grim mirrors at the gym. She talked to her therapist about calming self-talk. She wrote out a hierarchy of fear on the back of a red-paper menu at the cafe near her apartment. She bought a leather passport holder, decided which dress was luckiest to fly in, choosing a brown cotton knee-length with sky-blue birds embroidered around the hem. She stashed travel-size tubes of Tylenol, ginger candies and hand sanitizer into the front pocket of her backpack.

As you drive west the world opens up, the same way it does in Canada. The mountains and sky grow bigger until Teprine feels like a baby spider in a bathtub. She is not transformed. She can't write an inspiring memoir about overcoming the adversity of her agoraphobic tendencies. The disappointment feels worse than she imagined it would.

They have tried to break up, but they can't stop having sex. Teprine has two patchy bruises on her inner elbow from a blood test. She didn't want to get sick in America, so she got every test. If she were rich she'd request a full-body PET scan every few years. The nurse said her veins are impossible. She doesn't like to contemplate the existence of veins. Basic biology in grade nine made her gag. She can barely register that she lives inside a body. She and Jasper have this in common. Their bodies become the whole point. On this trip, as at home, when they're not otherwise occupied, they are having sex. When she hears him unbuckling his belt, her mouth opens on its own, her back arches. Even if he's just changing quickly into swim clothes, the metal clink makes her body ready.

She doesn't like to lie on her back – at the doctor's office, in yoga class during meditation – it makes her feel like she could float away. But she longs to be underneath him, anchored.

In 29 Palms, in a pink adobe cottage, he held the bed frame above her head to keep it from banging against the wall, but it was unstoppable. She used to move all around the room when she fucked someone. Now she just wanted to be still, his full weight on top of her.

On their first morning of the trip, before they were really awake, they were fucking fast and frenzied, as though battling through disconnection. Teprine couldn't turn her brain off, it processed the many layers of what was occurring, even while her mouth was saying all the things he liked to hear, even while her body was responding.

She wants to be someone for whom sanity is not something laboured for, the kind of person who can be present in every moment, who can walk into the desert with some water and a map and a sense of adventure, whose only concern is an excellent photograph. Faced with the unfamiliar, she's stuck in full histamine flutter.

But in a hotel bed, the new and the familiar collide. He has all the control in this game, she feigns helplessness. She never tires of his commanding voice, his soft theatrical coercion, his hand over her mouth.

There's a freedom in the constraint.

Two hours before their departing flight, he'd thrown a hitch in the plan.

'I love you,' he'd said, 'but something is missing.'

There wasn't a word for it, but it was missing. He'd rubbed his chest in a circular motion.

'Be more specific,' Teprine had said, though she didn't need him to be. Everyone knows when they're being broken up with, however kind and vague the rejection, even if it happens right after he makes you come thirteen times in a row in the back of his Mazda 5 in the Park 'N Fly lot by the airport.

'I love you,' he'd repeated, as if that made it significant. She'd furrowed her brow, then smoothing down her skirt she'd lifted the wrapper from a child's granola bar off her thigh like a Band-Aid. She had non-returnable tickets. She had a goal: to walk into the desert and stay alive.

'I still want you to come on this trip,' he'd said. She knew the thing to do, if she were a strong and independent woman, or the narrator in an anthemic R & B song, was to strut out of that Mississauga parking lot and into her own good-enough life. But she didn't cancel the trip.

'I guess it'll be like our farewell tour,' she'd said. She was angry but compared to her fear, her rage was more of an irritant than a serious problem.

At departures, he did his weekly shot of testosterone in the bathroom before they went through security. He claimed to not notice any differences, but every time he did it, his grip on her wrists tightened.

It goes without saying that Teprine is not a good flyer. Agoraphobics never are. Thankfully, Ativan engenders a feeling of being absent from the cruelties of the self. After dissolving one milligram under her tongue, Teprine was able to board the plane to Arizona.

She had a moment of clarity while sitting beside Jasper in the O'Hare departure lounge on a stopover: this was their last trip together. It was an almost neutral thought. A fact. Sometimes she gets a glimpse of her real personality while taking anti-anxiety medication. Perhaps underneath the screaming blur of all the irrational fear, she's actually pretty chill.

They didn't even get a chance to unpack their bags in the hotel room before his breath on her neck became urgent, and he'd whispered, 'You're mine,' and those words buoyed her against every known uncertainty.

Teprine will turn forty on the day they arrive in Los Angeles. Forty felt like a relief to Jasper. Everyone who already has kids says turning forty is a relief, but Teprine finds little solace in the tins of cream meant for the infinitesimal area under each eye. She wishes time could pause. When she sees babies, she sometimes voluntarily cries out with longing, and has to pretend it's just a coughing fit.

A week before the trip, Jasper's four-year-old looked at Teprine with weird toddler solemnity while she was reading him a bedtime story and said, 'When the end of the world comes, I'm going to dig a hole for my family. And you can come, too.' Teprine laughed and then went to the bathroom to cry because she knew she probably wasn't going to be around for another birthday, let alone the apocalypse.

Jasper appears, to Teprine, both scared of their relationship and scared of not being in their relationship. As soon as the break-up is final, he reaches for her all day long. She's not sure how she should react so she lets her body make the decision.

They stop along Route 62 at a series of giant dinosaur sculptures. She takes photos of him pretending to be eaten by the Tyrannosaurus rex. He texts the pictures to his kids. She looks around at the small grouping of desert houses and wonders if she should just put an end to the trip and rent an apartment. She could be one of the girls in flimsy dresses selling pies at one of the bakeries along the highway. She could rename herself something simple like Jen. Jen drinks her iced hibiscus tea behind the counter at the bulk spice store. She could settle down. Jen could be easy-going.

Later that night he calls the kids. They critique the photos he sent. 'They're not real dinosaurs,' they say. 'You don't look scared enough.'

The first twenty steps are always the most difficult. It's when an agoraphobic will most likely turn around. Teprine left the guest house in Tucson on their second day, heading towards a bus stop a few blocks away. Even as the ground began to tilt, and she gripped the edges of her white sundress, she kept going. She got to the bench beside the bus stop. Exposure therapy only works if you keep going, travel up and down the arc of panic.

Her skirt rose up and she could see the beautiful bruises on her thighs. He doesn't like them. 'I don't want to hurt you, ever. I love you.' But she likes to see her resilience reflected back. The bus stop was across from a deserted schoolyard. The only people around were inside their cars. She tried to read an essay by Susan Sontag. She could only read one line: *Wherever people feel safe . . . they will be indifferent.*

What does it mean to accept your limitations? She looked out the bus window at the city, the fast-food outlets, the university campus. She would feel better if she went back to the guest house. Sometimes she feels jealous of people who frame their mental health issues as disability issues. But she feels that if you stay home, the agoraphobia wins.

A man got on the bus and stared at her tits for so long without stopping that she almost admired his singular focus. She clenched and unclenched all the muscles in her legs while counting and trying to breathe slowly, trying to turn so the man couldn't stare. As she shifted, so did his gaze. She got off the bus quickly, so the man wouldn't follow.

At the Sparkroot Cafe the baristas were femmes in vintage sundresses, tattooed arms, much like her dress, her arms. One of them ran a finger along the deer tattoo on Teprine's bicep and complimented it. Teprine sat at a table and opened her laptop. She stared at the title page of her manuscript in progress. The Bon Iver album played, the Blue Bottle coffee: all of it combined to mollify her against the unknown. She knew all of those tastes, the sound of those chord progressions.

She closed her laptop and opened the travel journal she'd packed, hoping to write about her transformative journey. Tomorrow I will be more adventurous, she wrote. Today I will get settled. But she knew that she'd simply come back to this cafe the next day, and sit at this table, and order the same thing.

Teprine tried to join Jasper at an academic talk on poetic embodiments at the university. The map didn't betray the length of city blocks. No one else was walking. She flagged a cab, and the driver said, 'In another month, you wouldn't be able to just stand there, flagging me down. You'd be dead. That's how hot it gets here. You should be more careful.'

She got a small jolt of pleasure from knowing that she'd taken a risk, even a dumb accidental one.

Fifteen years earlier Teprine had been so afraid to take the subway that she would slip a token into the slot, get halfway down the stairs to the platform and then turn around. She'd spent days in her apartment, leaving only when she absolutely had to. She'd felt doomed to a life of very little, a small-scale world. She went to a doctor at the university walk-in clinic and after a two-minute assessment was told that people with her condition either kill themselves or go on medication. She got a vial of yellow and white pills that made her mouth dry.

Teprine has been off SSRIs for a decade. But sometimes it comes back, like a virus, seeping in when things get overwhelming, or whenever she arrives in a new place.

Teprine thinks the B in LGBT is the most embarrassing letter in the acronym. Her ex-girlfriend, a butch, used to get upset about Teprine potentially leaving her for a trans guy. When she'd started dating Jasper, her ex returned some books to her house and said, 'I knew it. I knew you wanted to date a trans guy.' Jasper gets upset thinking about her dating a cis guy. When she dates cis guys, which isn't often, they are upset if they think about her becoming a real lesbian. She thinks about dating another femme, the way the younger queers do with their #femmeforfemme nameplate necklaces, but feels she is too old. Sex would always feel like play-acting, looking over her shoulder for the camera. It is possible there is no one she can date that wouldn't feel uneasy.

A study comes out that says bi women have terrible mental health. Teprine only reads the headline.

Though naturally disinclined towards activities that involve either, Teprine joins a group hike. A blond yoga enthusiast called Leslie wants them to stand with the saguaro cacti, as some sort of ritual. Teprine follows along, despite feeling like too much of an East-Coast cynic to appreciate the New Age intent of the exercise. The hike was suggested by Jasper's scholar friends, who are interesting and awkward. They wear expensive clothes, but something is always untucked or aloft. Glasses don't stay on their faces.

'I'm afraid of heights,' she tells Leslie, because it is easier to say than to explain that she is afraid of space and air. 'I may be slow or leave early,' she continues. Leslie offers her a warm smile. Sometimes just admitting her anxieties allows them to retreat.

'To let the cacti communicate,' Leslie says, 'stay still.'

They watch her being still, and slowly stop fidgeting and stretching to imitate her pose. When Teprine tries to stand still, she feels as though she remains in motion.

'Let's begin our trek. Try to listen for what the saguara are saying,' Leslie says.

No one else finds this instruction peculiar, and Teprine begins the ascent. If she stays far from the edge, she will feel grounded, so she hugs the hill. She imitates normal human walking, takes photos of the cacti, the view. She watches the faces of others express wonderment at their surroundings. She tries to make her face look like their faces.

She walks a little farther up the hill before she feels it start. It comes initially as an impulse to sit on the ground, even though she's wearing a short dress and everything in the desert looks like it would prickle or itch. She wants to get close to the earth even though it would render her a spectacle or cause concern. But she doesn't sit. She keeps walking, every step farther from her body as it moves.

Teprine walks faster than the group, as though trying to outrun her fear. She is thrilled to see a bench on the side of the mountain. A sign beside it asks that visitors sit and offer prayers. There is a makeshift altar beside the bench where people have left objects – brightly coloured dolls, photos of people who have died. There's a faded photocopy of the singer Mia Zapata affixed to the altar. She remembers how shocked she was hearing about Zapata's murder. Teprine liked to listen to her music while walking home from work after last call. She practiced her fight face to the soundtrack of her screaming vocals.

Teprine was occasionally followed home from work. One night she'd dropped a sweater as she ran from a pursuer, slamming her apartment door in the drunk man's face. He'd scratched at the door with his nails, a sad feral cat. In the morning she'd found him curled up on her doorstep, wrapped in her bright pink cardigan, sucking on the wool.

A snake zips under the bench. She pulls her legs up. She practises breathing slow and intentional, and then she keeps walking up the trail.

She's completely lost track of the group, if they are ahead or behind her. She stands still, trying to hear footsteps, camera shutters clicking. She only hears her own pulse in her ears. The saguaro don't sing or sway.

Make yourself seem bigger, the guidebook said, if you ever see a mountain lion. Teprine had read it out loud to Jasper in the car: 'It's vital to maintain eye contact.' He told her not to worry.

'We won't see a mountain lion,' he said, laughing.

He spoke with a certainty she envied.

The cougar is curled up, sleeping, comma-shaped, a breathing rock, when she walks around a corner. She is so distracted by the possibility of every kind of peril, Teprine doesn't take notice of this very real danger until it's ten feet away. A sudden intake of breath, a retreat. This would be funny to everyone I know. That I'm going to die this way. Ironic.

She could lie down and just offer herself. The worrying would be over. She stands so still. And there isn't even a noise to startle him, perhaps just the smell of her, the way she must always smell like fear. He wakes up.

She yells, lifts her arms. She is five feet tall. She tries to mimic a saguaro. Ordinary. She belongs here. Eye contact. It doesn't work. It isn't working. He walks towards her. She remembers that her eyes are shielded in oversized shades and she pulls them off, throws them into the wind. She stares him down. She has never stared so hard. She hears herself yell again and the yells echo. He retreats, at first like a slow-moving liquid and then, hearing the oncoming group of hikers behind her, at a furious clip. She watches him go. It looks like he's flying up the hill.

When Teprine was young and first suffering and didn't know why, she would do anything not to be alone, though the effort involved in being around people exhausted her. She would choose men and women she had nothing to say to, lying in their beds so that she wouldn't die alone in hers. She'd rather hold a cock in her hand for a few minutes than face certain suicide if she went home by herself. She thought about suicide not as an act she would participate in, but something that would happen to her. So she'd walk to the bar and order two drinks, just to make sure she had a witness. She needed a witness, so that she would keep her body together.

'You are so lucky to be alive,' says Leslie. She gathers Teprine in her arms. Her hair smells like carrot greens. 'That could have been it. That could have been all there was to your life,' she babbles.

That night Jasper whispers, 'I'm so grateful for you, I'm so grateful for you,' into her mouth, parting her legs with his knee.

In LA, they drive to Malibu, stretch towels along the sand and celebrate Teprine's birthday. At the beach it's as though they have crawled inside every film, every TV show, and they are imaginary. They rent a guest house in the backyard of a wealthy couple in the Palisades. At night, she becomes beautiful stillness, falling back into the sheets. He places one hand on her mouth, whispers, 'You're mine, forever. Forever.' She knows forever means one more day, one flight home. He exhales in a groan, all the beauty in that cool room. ∎

Scottish Wildlife Trust

On Wednesday, Jean helped protect osprey chicks.

On Thursday, she helped plant trees for red squirrels.

On Friday, she helped change the law to safeguard our land and seas.

On Saturday, it was five years since Jean passed away.

Make your wishes live on by writing us into your Will.

Jean's gift to the Scottish Wildlife Trust in her Will was a simple yet powerful way to keep her wishes alive.

You can do the same.

Once you've taken care of your loved ones, please consider including a gift to the Scottish Wildlife Trust in your Will. No matter how big or small, you can be sure it will make a difference to Scotland's wildlife.

To find out more call Zoë on 0131 312 4772 or visit scottishwildlifetrust.org.uk/legacy

Scottish registered charity (no. SC005792)

© BERTRAND DORNY
Central Park
Courtesy of Galerie Le Coin des Arts, Paris

JAILBAIT

Ottessa Moshfegh

The day before I left home for college, I made a phone call to the publishing house of a writer I'll call Rupert Dicks. Dicks had a reputation as one of the most audacious and brilliant minds in literature in the last century, and his work represented everything I held as sacred at the time – he was innovative, unapologetic and dedicated to the craft of honest prose. At seventeen, I knew I was a writer, and I wanted to know what Rupert Dicks knew. I was determined to get him to tell me.

'I'm calling because I'm a student of Rupert Dicks,' I told the book editor on the phone.

'I didn't know Rupert had any students at the moment.'

'Well, I'm his student. Mind asking him to call me?'

I was a kid, but I wasn't naive. A glance at Dicks's author photo had given me some insight into how I could talk my way into his tutelage.

'Tell him I'm a freshman at college,' I said to the woman on the phone. There, I thought. That'll get him. I gave her the phone number of my soon-to-be dorm room. When I moved in the next day, the red light on the answering machine was blinking.

'Rupert Dicks here. I understand you're interested in writing. I don't know what you look like or if you've got any talent, but give me a call and I can tell you what I think.'

I called him back. Without much chitchat, Dicks gave me directions to a particular bench in an enormous park on the other side of town, the site of our meeting the next morning.

'Bring your work,' he said. 'See you tomorrow.'

I was thrilled.

That afternoon, I went to college orientation, mingling with students who seemed, suddenly, like children. I had a secret, a path, and passion that would lead my life to interesting places, not just around the corner to the university library. If I felt any anxiety about my meeting with Dicks the next day, it was that he would refuse to teach me or tell me my work was juvenile.

'Let's see what you've brought me,' Dicks said when we met. No hello, no handshake. He hunched over on the bench, took out a pen, and started drawing diagonal lines across every page of the story I'd given him. I sat down next to him and surveyed him. He wasn't a large man, but his body vibrated with the demanding neediness of a man who had once been very beautiful and powerful. At sixty-five, he now had age spots on his face, jowls, thin white hair edging out from under his hat. I remember thinking his waning vitality could be used to my advantage. If I succeeded in reflecting his great masculine strength, then he'd want me around, might take more of an interest in my work, tell me more, explain more, enlighten me more.

'So?'

'There's a garbage can over there,' Dicks said nonchalantly. He seemed to want this to hurt my feelings, although it did not. I took the pages from his fingers and crumpled them up, made two baskets into the garbage can, but missed on the third. I stood and bent down to pick up the balled-up paper, knowing Dicks would have a perfect view of my butt. It was innocuous, and yet very deliberate.

'Let's walk,' he said when I returned to the bench.

He talked for an hour about craft, curiosity, urgency, warned against the pitfalls of subconscious conformity, complacency and people-pleasing. I tried not to ask too many questions because they only inspired outrage and scorn. Along the way, he name-dropped writers and editors.

Finally, he turned to sex. I played along, but I was no Lolita. I was not sucking lollipops or sitting on anyone's lap. This was a game of egos. If I wanted what Dicks had to give me – the wisdom of his experience as a great writer – I would have to venerate him and lead him on, to flirt. But I couldn't seem too willing. If I didn't hold myself up high enough and play hard to get, my allure would vanish, along with his tutelage.

'Seventeen, eh? Jailbait,' he said. 'I should be careful what I do with you. And if you're ever famous, you could try to humiliate me. Which would be pathetic on your part. Women and their boohoos and neediness.'

Our first meeting concluded with a writing assignment. He told me to come back when I'd finished. I called him a week later.

'I did what you told me.'

'Good girl,' he said, and invited me to his apartment for the first of a handful of meetings over the course of the school year.

Dicks lived alone in a beautiful apartment decorated by his wife, who'd died years earlier. The whole place was dark. The kitchen, even on the sunniest day, was a cold chamber of shadows. Dicks and I sat across from each other, a small desk lamp on the kitchen table illuminating the printed pages I brought with me. At each meeting, he made me a martini. He ate cereal and smoked marijuana. Conversation was mostly one-sided: a man and his audience.

None of the work I showed him was very good, or very honest. But that was beside the point. I just wanted to listen to him talk. If he spent five minutes addressing my writing, I felt my visit was worthwhile. My ambition was not to be successful – to publish books and be renowned, rich and powerful, like Dicks; I wanted, truly, to use my writing to rise up to a higher realm of existence, away from the stupidity I saw in my classmates, teachers and parents, or on television and on the subway. I understood that life would be meaningless unless my art reached toward an understanding of who I was, and what I was doing here. I don't know if Dicks sensed my seriousness as a writer. Part of what made him interesting was that I felt he would dismiss me the moment I bored him. And he did, sometimes, tell me to leave abruptly, when he'd had enough. I kept calling and asking if I could visit. Dicks never refused.

When I turned eighteen, our meetings became more overtly sexual in tone. One day he took me by the hand and led me into his office, unearthed a huge cardboard box, and proceeded to pull out photographs, mostly Polaroids, of young, attractive women. 'These are some of the chicks I've laid,' he said. There were hundreds of them. 'I shouldn't have to convince you: I know what I'm doing in the sack.'

Another time, I raised my arms to lift a book off a high shelf and Dicks traced his finger over my exposed stomach. Nobody had touched me there before. 'You know, with age, the nerve endings in your fingertips become more sensitive. I can do more with this one finger than some college kid could do with his entire body.' He made a good case for himself. The touch lingered long enough for me to be stunned for a minute. I made up an excuse to leave quickly that day. But I called again before too long.

Then there was the kiss at his kitchen table. Sixty-five-year-old lips, cold, slack, weirdly passionless. I felt nothing. I can't say I wasn't disappointed. When he sat back down, he asked if he could take me to bed. He didn't want to have intercourse, he explained. He just wanted to pleasure me. I said no. We argued about this for hours. Yes, I stayed for hours and argued. They were some of the most rhetorically challenging hours of my life. I'd never been more present. I was alive and engaged, watchful and cautious with my body language, arrogant and flirtatious in my speech. Dicks mesmerized me. If I'd been any less determined as a writer, I may have been persuaded.

The last time I saw Dicks, I brought a new story. Dicks read it over my shoulder in the love seat in his immaculate bedroom. He edited the entire piece, explaining his reasoning for every move – it was a private masterclass, just what I'd always wanted. 'Thank you,' I said. 'This means so much to me.' Then Dicks went to his closet and began a show-and-tell of lubricant gels, dirty movies, contraceptive sponges, etcetera. So, we argued about sex again. None of it turned me on, not the argument, not his erotic devices, not him. He'd given me what I wanted, teacher to student. I didn't feel like paying him back.

'I'm sorry I've wasted so much of your time,' I said. 'I won't come back, I promise.'

Dicks was irate, and yet he helped me on with my boots.

'I have better things to do, you know, than muck around with some kid.'

That was the end.

At thirty-six, I'm pretty fluent in irreverence and cynicism. My assumption that people are ultimately self-serving lowers my expectations and allows me to forgive. More importantly, it empowers me to be selfish, and to cast off the delusion that I'll get what I want just by 'being nice'. We are all unruly and selfish sometimes. I am, you are, he is, she is. Like Dicks, I have little patience for small talk or politesse. One has to be somewhat badly behaved to write above the fray in a society most comfortable with palatable mediocrity. One has to be willing to upset the apple cart. Apples go flying, people trip and fall, yelp, grab for one another. A street corner is transformed into a tragic circus. And everybody gets an apple, each one bruised and broken in a special way. That's the kind of writer I have always wanted to be, a troublemaker. I can't fault Dicks or anyone else for wanting the same. ■

TERRY FROST
Black Moon and Ochre, 1997
© The estate of Sir Terry Frost, Courtesy of Flowers Gallery

THAT

Leni Zumas

B efore you tell me it was inappropriate to contact you, before you remind me it all happened a long time ago, before you suggest I'm embittered by my lack of success – have you heard all the facts?

A decade ago I enrolled in a low-ranked graduate program in creative writing at a Midwestern university. The annual tuition and fees totaled $18,666. I received no funding from the school. My mother earned $26,000 a year. I got a job at the Dining Commons and took out a student loan, which, ten years later, I am nowhere close to paying off.

It was not my first loan. I still owed plenty on what I'd borrowed for undergrad. I'd heard that if you went back to school, you could pause the monthly payments on existing debt. And my secret wish was to be a writer. I can't remember what shape, exactly, ambition made inside me; but I knew I had some, and it was thrilling.

Members of the committee, I am bitter, it's true. But this doesn't change the facts.

M y first term in the program, I was too scared to register for a fiction workshop. I fulfilled my literature requirements instead. I kept my studio apartment clean. I made the loan money stretch farther by stealing food during my shifts at the Dining Commons – not difficult, once I figured out who could be trusted. I went days without speaking to anyone except my salad-station customers, most of them girls. I watched them register the disharmony between me and the celery, me and the spinach leaves. How could someone who looked like *that* sell salad? wondered their slender, wilting brains.

In December I stocked up on dry goods (nuts, cereals, tortilla chips) to get me through winter break.

Spring term, I forced myself to take a workshop. Ten of us sat in a circle while Professor Sedgwick paced the perimeter or stood at the blackboard, chalking rules: REFRAIN FROM THE GIVENS and IF YOUR NERVE, DENY YOU – GO ABOVE YOUR NERVE – . Thaddeus, as he told us to call him, was a tall white man with sandy hair cut short above a high, smooth forehead. He looked like a surfer too long away from the sun.

The first story I submitted was about a woman who tries to count every hair on her body. It began: 'Pluck three hairs from the loaf of your pubis. Put them on your tongue. A not-now girl's hair tastes more mineral than a not-yet's.'

Thaddeus hated the story. It reeked of the precious, he said – pathology du jour – and I had a terrible command of hyphenation.

R omy and I lived in the same rotten apartment building. She was a second-year, full of advice. Make sure to take Professor Unthank's Poetry of Horror class. Don't walk past the frat houses after dark. Don't let Thaddeus pay for your drinks after workshop at the Swan with Two Necks.

'Although you won't have to worry,' she said.

'Why?'

'You're not – his type.'

'Which is?'

'Super-pretty, in, like, a delicate way? And brown.'

(Committee, I am white.)

'Did he buy *your* drinks?'

'I'm not delicate,' Romy said.

'You are delicate!'

'Girl, please.'

Romy was thirty but wore her black hair in pigtails wrapped with twist ties, and went around in a coat made of fake rabbit fur. She was from Los Angeles and (she confessed one night when drunk) kind of rich. *'Kind of* rich?' I tried not to seem angry, because I wanted us to be friends. She hadn't received funding either, but it was no problem for her parents to cover the tuition and fees. They would have helped her rent a nice apartment, but Romy had insisted on the Lion Arms because she wanted the experience of living in a shithole. Her grandparents (she said before throwing up a little, into her hand) worked themselves to the bone in code-violating restaurants so that she could choose to live in a shithole.

I checked Thaddeus's first novel, *Lategoers*, out of the library. It was neither terrible nor good. (I haven't read his newest, the one getting all the 'buzz'). Then I churned out twenty-two pages of something similar.

> She reached for the young deer as if to caress its tenderling, but instead of petting the antler bud she brought her fist down onto it. When the brothers came home, pissed as Baptists, they found the animal dead on the yard stones.

I added a few of my own swerves and flourishes for disguise, and called the story 'I Will Make You Regret It'. Though it wasn't due for another week, I emailed it to Thaddeus. *Would love to hear your thoughts, before I distribute?*

The next day he left the following letter in my department mailbox:

Dear Eleanor,

Bravo. Just bravo.
Or is it brava, in your case? I can't remember and am too drunk to locate a dictionary, ha, joking, I'm not (too) drunk but the wind is up and the bald cypress are shaking like the devil's seeds, which keeps me at the typewriter. I see no need to give you any so-called feedback, any bloodless little grocery list of omissions and errors: because your story is beautiful. I'm sort of in love with your story. I come from the mountains, too, did you know that? I come from people who can't pronounce 'banal'. When your narrator says, 'Leave me to myself in the hollow,' I know precisely what the hell she means. I read a few paragraphs to my wife. She's a lowlander but was impressed all the same. Can we meet to talk about this marvel?

Ever yours,
Thaddeus

The sentence 'I'm sort of in love with your story' thrust a wet wire deep into my chest, where it sizzled and twitched.

At the bottom of the letter he'd added, in red pen: 'Not at the Swan. Mind coming to chez Sedgwick? Sat 5 p.m.?' He typically held conferences at the Swan with Two Necks, because his campus office smelled like work and as for meeting in a coffee shop – what were we, teenagers?

I took a bus to an outskirts neighborhood with lawns and no sidewalks. Thaddeus's address was a sweet-looking bungalow situation. He had mentioned in class that the house was a rental. I found out later it was owned by Thaddeus's wife – who had a name, though I never once heard him use it.

He opened the door in his pale blue sweatshirt, jeans and bare feet. 'Hey, hey. Come on back. You want a beer?'

'No thank you.'

On our quick march through the dining room, I saw a wall of photographs, all of the same red-haired, narrow-faced woman. Thaddeus was hugging her in a few of the shots, but mostly it was just the woman, this stern white flamingo, apparently conceited enough to want fifty versions of herself on display.

Beyond the kitchen was a glassed-in porch, where a typewriter rested on a butcher block, facing a yard of crooked trees.

I sat on the hard pink wadding of a wicker sofa. My teacher straddled an office chair, swiveled to face me, and rested his chin on the chair-back.

'You wrote such a beautiful story,' he said.

'Thanks,' I said.

'I mean, holy *fuck*, Eleanor. It hits on all sixes. So much better than your Anne-Carson-in-a-locked-ward nonsense. Where you from?'

'Monroe County, Ohio.'

He grinned. 'A fellow Appalachian.'

'Yep,' I said.

'Whereabouts, exactly?'

'Near Graysville?'

Thaddeus nodded. The chair was so close I could make out the white star at the center of a red pimple above his eyebrow.

He said, 'I'm going to nominate you for the Cravaack.'

'Seriously?'

'If you're from Monroe County, I know you've never seen that kind of money in your life.' The Cravaack Prize is $10,000. 'Whereas all those Shitty von Shatsteins in your cohort – like, what's his name, Zach?' Thaddeus shook his head. 'You hear he just bought a new Prius? Factory-fresh? That kid is fucking twenty-three! My dad paid our rent in cash. Every month. Didn't trust banks, so he kept his money in the chest freezer.'

'Smart,' I said, thinking of Romy's face: *By the way? I won the Cravaack.*

Thaddeus frowned. 'I also hope, Eleanor, that you're able to understand your weight problem in the context of poverty. It's a systemic epidemic, not just individual weakness. I saw it all the time back home. God, the stigma. Being fat and poor, as a woman? You're double-fucked.'

I am typing this part slowly, wishing to nail each word to the page exactly as it came out of his mouth. When I made my statement to the university lawyer, I spoke slowly. *Being fat and poor.* She taped it on a whirring recorder. *As a woman.*

'I'd like to see you harness that pain,' Thaddeus continued. 'The double-fuckedness. You *gesture* at it but never *go* there. What does it feel like, for instance, to be sitting here across from a six-foot-two adult male with good muscle tone, and know that you weigh more than he does?'

I stared at him.

'Not a rhetorical question,' he said. 'What does it feel like?'

I shrugged.

By the way I won the Cravaack. Won the Cravaack won the Cravaack.

'If you're going to be an artist, you cannot be afraid of shit like this.' Thaddeus yawned and clasped his hands together, stretched his arms out in front of him. The interlaced fingers came to rest on my right shoulder.

What had happened to all the words I knew?

The fingers were pressing, thudding, into my collarbone. His pale blue sweatshirt sleeve smelled of the same detergent my mother used.

Won the Cravaack.

He said softly, leaning forward, 'Do mountain girls like it vertical?'

I lowered my shoulder until the fingers slid off. 'Sorry, but, um.'

'God, *joking*.' He swiveled away, slapped his palms on the butcher block. 'Your title is melodramatic. Change it before you pass out copies to the class, okay?'

He was staring through the glass at the bald cypress. I pulled on my coat and left.

Having missed the last bus into town, I had to walk for nearly an hour. My mouth tasted like blood. The taste was worth it, I decided, because of the nomination. My entry would be due soon. I'd need to come up with a new title, and maybe cut the part about raccoons being ground up in the diner's burger meat.

'What the fuck, girl?' Romy stood on the front steps of the Lion Arms, in her fake rabbit coat. She took one last suck of a cigarette and threw it on the frozen lawn. 'Your face is weird. Are you crying?'

'It's sweat,' I said.

'It's like ten degrees out.'

'I was exercising. Pardon me.' I stepped around her, brought out my key.

'Good night?' she yelled after me.

I kept the Cravaack to myself for days – did not even call my mother. I wrote generous comments on Zach's workshop story. I went shopping in an actual supermarket, picking out things you couldn't get at the Dining Commons: clove-studded chocolate, artichoke hearts, pesto in a tube. After I had paid for my delicacies, I steered outside and waited while a woman with gray curls and a neon pink visor tried to nudge her cart back into the row. It refused to fit. Kept snagging, misaligning.

I finally said, 'You need to really slam it.'

'I will not do violence,' she muttered, backing away.

I slammed hers and mine in together.

On the first warm day of spring, headed to campus under a flame-blue sky, I told Romy the news. She stopped walking. Squinted at the air right above my head.

'Is a professor allowed to nominate more than one student?'

'No,' I said.

'Oh.'

'What?'

A small, stony laugh came out of her. She swung her arms in big circles until her backpack fell off. Stooping to retrieve it, she said, 'He nominated me, too.'

'But – that's not possible.'

Romy shrugged. 'He cc'ed me on the email to them.'

I had not been cc'ed on any goddamn email.

'For the *nurse* novel?'

'Try not to sound shocked as fuck, Eleanor.'

The discussion of my story, whose title was now 'Tenderling', lasted barely half an hour. Thaddeus said nothing at all – a signal to my classmates they were free to pile on.

'I'm troubled by the stereotyping of Appalachian culture.'

'Okay, so the deer's symbolic, but of *fucking what?*'

'This feels kind of derivative.'

I stared at the fingers that had rested on my shoulder. All the nails on his left hand had crescents of brown dirt under them. The right-hand nails were clean. Thaddeus didn't wear a wedding ring, because artists had a duty to refrain from the givens.

Romy pointed out the beauty of certain images, such as the bruised antler bud and the narrator counting the wings of dead flies while she crouched in her hiding place. But before she could cite a third example, Thaddeus cut in: 'I think we've said what needs to be said. Let's call it a night. I'll be posting up at the Swan, if anyone wants to join.'

'The first assignment you turned in for Professor Sedgwick's class,' said the university lawyer, glancing down at a thickness of papers, 'involved the consumption of pubic hair. Did you intend for this to be provocative?'

'As in thought-provoking?'

'As in sexually.'

'Just because the hair is near a sexual organ doesn't mean it's sexual hair.'

'Okay, calm down,' said the lawyer. 'I have to ask.'

I was calm, except at the salad station, where the knife kept slipping. Some blood found its way onto the corn niblets. I thought the red drops relieved the boredom of the yellow, but my supervisor did not agree.

There was no official investigation. The university lawyer scheduled a 'conciliation session' at which Thaddeus and I sat at either end of a huge, shining table. The lawyer sat at one of the long sides, with a tape recorder, and some sort of dean was hunched on a stool by the door.

I explained, again, what had happened.

Fat and poor. Fingers. Not a very friendly mountain girl.

Thaddeus, who had not even dressed up – who had come in his goddamn blue sweatshirt – looked at the lawyer, then looked at me.

Do you sincerely believe, his gaze seemed to say, I would force myself on *that*?

The lawyer coughed.

Sweat gushed down my rib cage, into the creases, every hair drowned and uncountable.

Members of the committee, have any of you ever been *that*?

No matter what the dean's internal memo claims, I did inquire, at the conciliation session, about filing charges. At which point the lawyer said, 'According to Professor Sedgwick, you were threatening him. You were angry that he didn't nominate you for the award.'

'Not true.' I looked at Thaddeus, who looked back at me with zero expression.

'The professor has provided us with a copy of an email he received, dated March fourth of this year.'

The lawyer walked around the table to hand me a piece of paper, on which was printed the email to which I'd attached my second workshop story. Except there was no attachment, and no message. There was only the subject line – 'I Will Make You Regret It' – above an empty body, a block of throbbing white.

'This was sent from your university account.'

'Oh my God,' I said.

'So you see . . .' The lawyer tucked the paper back into its manila folder.

Before you tell me it's my own fault for not protesting harder, for not making the lawyer understand – do you think I don't already know that?

Thaddeus Sedgwick grew up, I have since discovered, in New Jersey. Kittatinny Mountain may technically belong to the Appalachian Range, but its residents can get to a Manhattan restaurant in less than two hours.

And I am from Cincinnati: hilly, but hardly mountainous.

My mother picked me up at the airport in her rattling Jeep with the I CAN GO ON A DIET BUT YOU'LL BE UGLY FOREVER! bumper sticker.

When we hugged, I smelled Thaddeus in her purple fleece vest.

'That's a lot of luggage,' she said.

'I'm back for good.'

I reached for the Minnie Mouse sunglasses she kept in the glovebox and put them on. My explanation was true as far as it went: I had left the program because it was too expensive.

I didn't mention my teacher, or what I'd done to Romy.

The day before I dropped out of grad school, I walked to campus to return all my books. The fines had begun to mount. On a bench outside the library sat a woman who looked a lot like the photos in Thaddeus's house: blotchless white skin, red hair in a ponytail, body thin to the point of *Hmmm*. The bell-bottoms of her black dress pants flapped in the prairie wind.

I went up and asked for the time.

The lowlander raised her eyes from her phone. 'Almost five.' Noticing my three plastic bags, strained to bursting: 'Don't worry, you'll make it.'

'Thanks so much.' I kept standing there.

'Anything wrong?'

'Sorry,' I said. 'You just look familiar.'

'Well, I teach here.'

'Does your husband teach here, too?'

Her face tightened. 'I don't have a husband.'

'Oh, I'm sorry. I mean – not sorry that you don't have a husband, but –'

'Got it,' she said, and stood up and walked away.

A bed of my own making, one therapist called it.

'You invited special attention from your professor by all but plagiarizing his work; you claimed a false regional identity; you spread a vindictive rumor about your best friend sleeping with your professor in exchange for a prize nomination.'

'She wasn't my *best* friend –'

'Can you choose to see your complicity here, Eleanor? Your own role in this drama?'

'Um, what?' I said to the therapist I would choose never to see again.

The committee may fault this letter for its omissions. I have not, for instance, described myself. I have not invited the reader into the sensations of this mooring of flesh – what it feels like to live as *that*. But why, in fact, should I bother? Why make the effort to narrate my body, to name its terms and conditions, when the rest of the world is happy to do it for me?

'You would look cuter,' Romy once said, 'in vertical stripes.'

'Horizontal's my thing,' I told her.

She didn't win the Cravaack that year, but she managed to publish, in a small magazine called *Textscraper*, the first chapter of her novel about student nurses in Los Angeles. In the draft we read for workshop, the villain was a spiteful anesthesiologist known as Jimmy. In the published version, the anesthesiologist's name is Eleanor.

Members of the committee, do you know what it feels like to be fucked if you do and double-fucked if you don't? I'm aware of your names and credentials, but not whether, or how much, you care about the facts. Your book prize, one of the nation's most prestigious, pays more than the Cravaack but less than what I owe on my student loans. Among the current finalists is Thaddeus Sedgwick, and I am wondering what can be done to correct this.

Before you say stop lecturing us, bitter fat girl, stop gnawing your twig of resentment, stop blaming your debt and obesity and failure to publish on a talented novelist who's finally getting his due – let me ask you: should it matter that I'm not as sympathetic a character as one might hope? That I'm even, dare I say, *off-putting*? A victim is supposed to be virtuous. A damaged angel. Would it be easier to decide what to do about Thaddeus if you had a better idea of how damaged I am?

I still live in Cincinnati, where I work at Buckeye Coffee, or the DMV. I have three children, or I am childless. My cats adore me, or my cats are all dead. Did I stop writing fiction altogether? Do I create social media aliases so I can keep track of Romy and Thaddeus and Prius-buying Zach? I guess I don't think it matters so much who *I* am. That is: what if I'd gone on to wild literary success? What if I were stomping through the book world like a goddamn queen? Would that change what Thaddeus did?

There's one fact you can be sure of. My favorite part of the week, the moment I'm happiest and most myself, is at the grocery store, when I return my shopping cart to its metal-railed slot.

When I shove it as fast and as hard as I can. ∎

Momtaza Mehri

Biscotti Boys / On Men Who Wear Living as Loosely as Their Suits

salmaan the second son & his mama's seventh seal by way of
  underwater & underemployment

by way of the coastal regions where boys become men become
  gone too soon

or never soon enough

his only son now has water on the brain

heard you didn't have to pay so much for treatment here

a gamble that cost all the gold in his wife's closet

on odd-numbered holy night

he prays for deliverance for damnation for the divine miracle of
  drosophila

for a better dunya

ibraahim by way of fake papers by way of ain shams by way of two
  years

of exhaust fumes & switchblades

by way of engine oil thick as lust & thieves the street beggars having
  less but always enough

to know he is less

they need no documentation to be sure of this

no jawaaz no passport no waraaqo

           the dark of his greasy calves is proof enough

BISCOTTI BOYS / ON MEN WHO WEAR LIVING AS LOOSELY AS THEIR SUITS

uthman by way of motown mustache by way of mombasa crackle

the first to leave

now has a summer home & a second wife a few cousins in the
   camps but here

here he has a maid who cannot read the payslips she receives

here is not over there where the kids are hyphenated & disrespectful

& always breaking your heart

here is where he can hold his head up high & feel like a man

you must understand to feel like a man is something worth traveling
   for

                              is something worth drowning for

Grace Paley, 2000
© CHRIS FELVER / GETTY IMAGES

WHAT DO WOMEN WANT?

READING GRACE PALEY AFTER #TIMESUP

Devorah Baum

In 1974, the year I was born, Grace Paley published a short story called 'Wants' – you can find it freely online. The story is one of renewal and it's one that I return to often even though its characters and concerns – women and men, women who love men – might seem to some old-fashioned. It never gets old for me.

The story is two and a half pages long. Paley's stories were all short, she once explained, because she was a woman with more wishes and responsibilities than those of a writer alone. She was also a mother, a daughter, a wife, a friend, an activist, a citizen. Pressed with such demands her time, inevitably, was limited. And 'Wants' is a story not only engaged with what a woman wants, but with a woman's time: with what her wants and her time might have to do with each other.

It begins with our narrator sitting on the steps of the 'new library' and seeing her ex-husband in the street. 'Hello, my life, I said. We had once been married for twenty-seven years, so I felt justified.' A wry, melancholic but nonetheless friendly opening is thus oddly concluded with the sort of inward justification that alerts us to what machinations may have dissolved their marriage: accusations, ripostes, words always barbed, braced, ready for the next charge. And indeed our narrator is met with an instant rebuff: 'What? What life? No life of mine,' which she quickly accommodates: 'I said, OK.

I don't argue where there's real disagreement.'

In my own marriage, my reluctance to argue where there's real disagreement has itself been a source of real disagreement. It's not hard to see why. When I fall silent or turn coolly compliant in the midst of a heated discussion I'm often accused of withdrawing into a cold frigidity or passive aggression. And to the extent that I am, like Paley's narrator, inwardly constructing my own unstated justifications, there's certainly such a case against me to be made. But there may still be a case to be made for refusing to make my case. Because who wants one's marriage to be a battlefield where positions must always be established and sides defended or attacked until a victor has been declared?

Introducing *What Do Women Want?* (1983), co-authors Susie Orbach and Luise Eichenbaum quote the sociolinguist Deborah Tannen: 'Boys and girls grow up in what are essentially different cultures, so talk between women and men is cross-cultural communication.' Sexual stereotypes regarding styles of discourse have tended to hinge on the idea of women chasing conversation in the hope of connection and intimacy, while men are supposedly looking to trade information, solve problems and bring unnecessary chatter to a close. (There are punning parallels to be made here to stereotypical notions of what drives female versus male sexuality, too.) When women make it known that they want to 'talk', for example, and yet, men quickly discover, this talking may be open and meandering with no obvious content, direction or end in sight, that's when men can predictably turn an exasperated cartoon shrug to the camera: *you see how impossible they are, how there's nothing I can do to mollify them ... what on earth do women want?*

This is pretty much the run of things in my own household. What we're arguing about turns out to be how to speak to each other at all. What is conversation good for? Arguments at least appear to have a sense of direction, and yet an argument, even if won or lost, tends to preserve the disagreement in some form, which may be the inevitable outcome of any kind of intercourse that's been declared decisively 'over' – see also, the history of war. So while arguments can seem a noble quest to bring disagreements out in the open, and hence to an end, it's equally possible that arguments are provoked by an anxiety *about* endings. Arguing may be an attempt to ward off the unpredictability of endings by calling time on time.

When thinking about conversation, it's worth considering a type of conversation informed by a built-in reflection on its own purposes: the psychoanalytic session. The psychoanalyst D.W. Winnicott once observed that session endings can be a way for the analyst to insinuate hostility towards their patients, even when those endings are consensual, amicable and agreed upon in advance. Discussing a case study of a female analyst who found it hard to end sessions with a particular client, a businessman, within the allotted fifty minutes, writer and analyst Anouchka Grose remarks that the female analyst suspects herself of having haplessly colluded with her client's wish for 'her to see him for love, not money' because of 'social conditioning around women and caring. She thinks a male therapist would find it easier to end the sessions.' Love as unwaged labour is meant to be the special domain of women, after all.

Do male therapists really find endings less vexing? Perhaps. Yet the psychoanalytic situation is also one that invites us to project sexual identities that have less to do with anatomy or social conditioning than with the fluid and transferable characteristics that make sharing possible. Gender, in other words, as a question of what position you're occupying in a particular discourse – such as who is doing the talking and who the listening. In my own case, for example, I know I've certainly tried pushing back the finishing line of sessions with my male analyst. Asking myself why, it's as if I've been protesting the way in which 'time's up' forces me to reckon with the economic nature of our relations. So isn't it conceivable that, like the businessman, the mystery of what I really, really want (which I usually claim not to know) is no less bound up with a fantasy of what might be signified or promised by 'free time'? Hence too, no doubt, why I'm just as likely to be the first to announce when our time's up in the manner of someone pre-emptively ending a relationship before the other gets a chance to.

No matter the instigator, efforts to tie things up are frequently marked by a wish to close down a state of openness and uncertainty about what the other really wants; a state that's experienced as threatening. As such, it's not unreasonable to suspect that the patriarchal question 'what do women want?' might be posed by someone whose purported wish to know may be disguising their wish *not* to know. A question, after all, calls for an answer, but what if what 'women' want is a chance to speak or share unhampered by the demand that they get to the point? Indeed, this suggests why Freud, as happens so often, may be both the purveyor of the problem and its best response. For though it was he who made infamous the question, he's also the curator of a way of talking and being listened to that *doesn't* claim to know in advance what a conversation's ends are supposed to be. It's precisely the 'point' of psychoanalysis that talking can never really get to it.

In Paley's story, whatever arguments may have once brought this marriage to an end resume the moment the former spouses see each other again. So it makes sense that the story mostly takes place at the library's Books Returned desk, where our narrator has gone to return overdue books. For it's at this juncture that there occurs between our narrator and the librarian a conversation that mirrors the one she's having with her ex. Once again she's accused of a past misdemeanour. Once again she accommodates. 'I didn't deny anything. Because I don't understand how time passes' – an explanation we can accept, having just discovered that the so-called 'new' library is one to which she has owed these books for fully eighteen years. Indeed, one way of reading the story is as a sort of coming to (time) consciousness on the part of a narrator who has been stuck, unable to progress or move on. And since we know this to be the case with the books she's been unable to let go of, we can suspect the same about her ex-husband.

So what does it mean for someone to become conscious of time? Perhaps time-consciousness, in Frank Kermode's apt phrase, is simply the sense of an ending. A narrative sense, then, but also one that might awaken a kind of political sensibility that allows us to glimpse that the way things are does not require us to suppose that they correspond to any natural law that renders them inevitable, but rather to a set of relations and actors that have shaped them in the past and might shape them differently in the future. And one that, at its worst, arouses a fervid apocalypticism such that the end in sight looks a dead certainty.

In any case, given its hold over the imagination, the sense of an ending, while it may endow a sense of time passing, doesn't assume adherence to chronology. What the perils of a fateful trajectory primarily seem to inspire, in fact, is the wish to move backwards in time. Mostly we long to return to the past out of nostalgia: terror of the present, a horror at the way time changes things, or because the unknown future is frightening. Yet the past needn't solely be sought out for the security of what's known.

In 'Wants', his version of their story has a definite outline: their marriage ended because 'you never invited the Bertrams to dinner'. 'That's possible,' our narrator concedes. 'But really, if you remember: first, my father was sick that Friday, then the children were born, then I had those Tuesday-night meetings, then the war began. Then we didn't seem to know them anymore. But you're right. I should have had them to dinner.' Her version of what she was responsible for back then is thus both more all-encompassing and less plotted, in part because, as she shows, she had no time to notice time passing. Since busyness is rarely an acceptable excuse, however – the people we let down suspect that we *do* make time for the things we want – she admits her fault. Or does she?

While her admission sounds, on the surface, pretty peaceable, as an anticlimactic wind-up of so much history it also feels like an escalation. Indeed, for her ex, the uninvited Bertrams remain a debt still owed him, as if time was unable to heal the wounds that her lack of time inflicted. These two warring reactions – his aggressive one, her passive-aggressive one – are juxtaposed with that of the librarian who immediately 'trusted me, put my past behind her, wiped the record clean', once her fines are paid. So it's the lending library that offers a vision of what it might be like to feel free of the past. With books, she's forgiven. And what this inspires in the story is renewal. Our narrator at once renews the same two Edith Wharton novels she'd come to return, reflecting that though she read them long ago, 'they are more apropos now than ever'.

The books are *The House of Mirth* and *The Children*, both novels written fifty years before Paley's story, at a time when women were beginning to organise themselves politically by making their demands and wishes known.

So at the 'liberating' Books Returned desk, we're recalled to an earlier emancipatory moment, and to the period when the pace of change was accelerating for everyone, though for women, as Wharton showed, most especially. Indeed, the historical consciousness we find in Wharton's fiction suggests that women could begin representing their own desires once they'd become conscious of the desires of their time. And they became time-conscious in large part by reckoning with the conditions of their *own* desirability – by noticing, for instance, how their place in the marriage market, along with that of so many other consumer objects, was tied to a sense of their built-in obsolescence.

Despite her poverty, her rumoured wantonness and her wish for not only status and money, but love, *The House of Mirth*'s Lily Bart remains marriageable while young. All such prospects are lost to her, however, as she ages. While in *The Children*, a man in his late forties ceases to want the grown woman with whom he's been matched as he finds himself falling for a teenage girl – though it's the novel's irony that a man of means, leisure time and scant responsibilities possesses none of this girl's maturity ('Judith's never been a child – there was no time').

In our own times, predators are big news: elevated to the loftiest positions on the one hand, hearing their time's up on the other. Yet looking back over one hundred years of the women's movement, from the first wave of feminism, when Wharton was writing, to the second wave when Paley was finding her 'more apropos than ever', reminds us that these times are by no means the first in which women have sought to call time on the exploitative nature of heterosexual relations. Nor, as that history shows, does a rising consciousness of one's situation and a consequent determination to end it mean the future won't repeat the past. But we can still hope that the present clash in the ongoing battle of the sexes might afford its combatants a chance to pause, reflect and learn from their shared history. Not least because, if the sense of an ending calls forth a historical consciousness, it can cause us to question those things that may have passed previously unnoticed, by appearing inevitable, natural, obvious . . .

For instance: what do men want?

It looks all too obvious in the case of the older man predating a young girl – the most indecorous version of what it's often said men *really* want. But that charge not only unfairly smears all men, it also fails to probe, as Wharton did, the confusions that abide within stories of wanting. Because what if we were to turn Freud's question on its head and suppose that what both women *and* men want is *not* to know what they want; a chance to be surprised? On this account, the predatory male may desire the ingénue precisely for her fantasised ignorance. Though if he finds himself consistently chasing the new, believing that passion can only dull with familiarity, then he has mistaken his object. For in wanting the unknown but pursuing the unknowing, he encounters nothing new, but rather locates in another's sexual ignorance a means of shoring up his own narcissistic image – the image that an older woman threatens, by knowing too much.

In 'Wants', after watching our narrator renew the books she'd come to return, her ex-husband seems suddenly hopeful that he too might get a second chance. We sense this when he recalls a 'nice' time they had together at the beginning of their marriage. But his nostalgia only has the effect of renewing their disagreement:

That was when we were poor, I said.
When were we ever rich? he asked.
Oh, as time went on,

she says, they were a family that didn't want for anything. Which isn't his memory: 'I wanted a sailboat ... you didn't want anything.' It's the kind of line that sounds like it knows what it wants: to bring things to a close. Whereas our narrator, though her irony is unmistakable now, still keeps her line open: 'Don't be bitter,' she tells him, about that sailboat, it's 'never too late'. And 'with a great deal of bitterness' he, for the first time, agrees: 'I'm doing well this year and can look forward to better. But as for you, it's too late. You'll always want nothing.'

To win an argument, as we know, you must have the final word (and you must believe there *can* be finality in words). As such, he seals his victory by following word with decisive deed: 'I sat down on the library steps and he went away.'

Yet time, we find in 'Wants', can never be fully determined, no matter how decisively one tries to end things. Thus the ex-husband's judgement – 'for you, it's too late. You'll always want nothing' – only provokes where it intended to close down. 'Now, it's true, I'm short of requests and absolute requirements. But I do want *something*,' our narrator reflects, continuing to converse with herself even after he leaves. She wants, she realises, 'to be a different person', such as the type of person who returns library books on time. She'd wanted to be a good mother, an effective citizen, an ender of wars. She wanted and still wants love:

> I wanted to have been married forever to one person, my ex-husband or my present one. Either has enough character for a whole life, which as it turns out is really not such a long time. You couldn't exhaust either man's qualities or get under the rock of his reasons in one short life.

While *he* might think his wants are obvious, his reasons straightforward, on that there remains between them real disagreement. Soon after, this is how the story ends:

> Well! I decided to bring those two books back to the library. Which proves that when a person or an event comes along to jolt or appraise me I *can* take some appropriate action, although I am better known for my hospitable remarks.

So, it's a happy ending: she returns the books not only punctually, but ahead of time. Yet as endings go, it hardly sounds conclusive. There's a risk, for instance, that she could be lapsing back into the perverse logic of claiming to know too much about what has determined her own history. Because what changed her exactly? She implies it's her ex-husband's accusation of passivity that jolted her into appropriate action. But when we first encountered her on the steps at the beginning of the story she was already taking those overdue books back to the library. So even by then something had shifted.

She's also, as we discover only towards the story's end, already remarried, which puts a somewhat different complexion on the matter of who has stayed stuck in the past and who has managed to move on. In which spirit too, perhaps, we can encounter the 'hospitable remarks' our narrator claims she's 'better known for'. For what are we to make, in the end, of the conversational style we've been observing throughout the story via her various acquiescences and accommodations for the sake of non-confrontation? One possible implication is that this putatively feminine style has been vanquished by the classical motif of man's propensity for heroic action – action that depends on knowing exactly what one wants. But since it's those open and inviting 'hospitable remarks' that are the story's actual last words, a question, is left hanging as to which of these behaviours – action or conversation – has been the real agent of change. Because isn't hospitality, as a form of admission, of letting others in, the more likely, in the long run, to make a lasting difference to a disagreeable situation? Viewed accordingly, refusing to argue where there's real disagreement, while it *can* be a cover for aggression, may also be a way of playing for time: the time it takes, for example, for real changes to emerge, or the free time beyond the finishing line when relations, being no longer subordinated to the laws of instrumental reason or economic exchange, seem fashioned not for money, but for love.

#TimesUp, these days, in part because there's seldom been more grotesque proof of patriarchal oppression than President Trump. But since Trump is not a man of reason, no argument can topple him. This is something Trump seems to have grasped early on when claiming at one of his rowdier campaign rallies: 'I could stand in the middle of Fifth Avenue and shoot somebody and I wouldn't lose any voters.' He might be right. As a man whose aggressions and appetites appear open and unapologetic, many of his supporters have thrilled to his transgressions. Much as, no matter how much he lies, his brashness has an air of frankness for those who perhaps feel they've been suffering for too long under an abstruse system of political correctness that has not allowed them to say what they think, do what they like or want what they want.

It's hardly surprising, then, that Trump excites people, arousing, as he does, not only the fanatical ardour of many who say they want him, but the impassioned disgust of those who say they don't. So it's worth pondering whether this frenzied 'love him or loathe him' fascination for Trump can tell us something about what we all might want. Or to put it more provocatively, what if, when it comes to predator Trump, it's we, his audience, who are the real predators, perversely relocating our deepest want – for less certainty about who we are, how we got here and what we ultimately want – onto the altogether unknowing? What we may have fallen for, in other words, could be ignorance. Although ignorance of the wrong kind. For Trump, as witnessed in his nostalgic and vengeful distortions of history, can offer nothing new, no hope, only despair. But even a mistaken object of desire can suggest something of what it is we might really want. So what we perhaps want, at a time when there seems no time to waste, not for any of us, not even for the millennial young, is another way of wanting, another way of experiencing time passing, another way of writing history.[1]

'There is a roof on our language that holds down our love,' George Saunders has written. 'What has put that roof there? Our natural dullness, exacerbated by that grinding daily need to survive. A writer like Paley comes along and brightens language up again, takes it aside and gives it a pep talk, sends it back renewed, so it can do its job, which is to wake us up.' It's the idea of literature as a space of hospitality. And in a world like ours, where disagreements are raging, stances are hardening, and where in both private and public, in both sex and politics, an atmosphere of intimidation stalks whoever fails to know in advance exactly what positions to take, it's a blessed relief to imagine there's still somewhere we can go that remains open, accommodating, ready to admit new possibilities. Every time I return to 'Wants' I read it differently. On every reading I find it timely. But it's a story that strikes me as more apropos now than ever. ■

---

[1] In an essay contrasting perversion and desire, Adam Phillips suggests these two forms of wanting give onto different 'ways of writing history' (see 'The Uses of Desire' in *One Way and Another*).

CONTRIBUTORS

Devorah Baum is Associate Professor in English Literature at the University of Southampton. She is the author of *Feeling Jewish (A Book for Just About Anyone)* and *The Jewish Joke*, and co-director of the documentary feature film *The New Man*.

Fiona Benson's full-length collection, *Bright Travellers*, received the 2015 Seamus Heaney Centre Prize for First Full Collection and the 2015 Geoffrey Faber Memorial Prize. Her second book, *Vertigo & Ghost*, will be published in 2019.

Tara Isabella Burton's debut novel, *Social Creature*, was published in June this year. She holds a DPhil in Theology from Trinity College, Oxford, and is currently the religion and faith correspondent for Vox.com. She has written for *National Geographic*, *1843* and the *Wall Street Journal*.

Paul Dalla Rosa is a writer based in Melbourne, Australia. His work has appeared in the *Lifted Brow*, *Meanjin* and *NY Tyrant*. He is currently undertaking a PhD at RMIT University on 'realness' in contemporary fiction.

Stella Duffy is an award-winning writer, playwright and stage performer, as well as the co-director of the Fun Palaces campaign for cultural democracy.

Fernanda Eberstadt is the author of five novels and *Little Money Street*, a non-fiction account of Roma families in France.

'I Bite My Friends' is a chapter from a forthcoming work.

Debra Gwartney is the winner of the 2017 River Teeth Literary Nonfiction Prize for the memoir *I'm a Stranger Here Myself* (forthcoming in 2019), and the author of *Live Through This*. Her work has been published in *Tin House*, *American Scholar*, the *Normal School*, *Prairie Schooner* and elsewhere. She teaches in the MFA programme at Pacific University and lives with her husband in Oregon.

Sébastien Lifshitz's documentary *Bambi*, a portrait of one of the first French transsexual women, won the 2013 Teddy Award at the 63rd Berlin International Film Festival. *Mauvais Genre*, the exhibition he curated on cross-dressers was featured at the Photographers' Gallery in London in 2018.

Andrew McMillan's debut collection, *physical*, was the first poetry collection ever to win the *Guardian* First Book Award. His new collection is *playtime*, a Poetry Book Society recommendation for Autumn 2018. He is senior lecturer in the Manchester Writing School, at Manchester Metropolitan University.

Momtaza Mehri is a poet and essayist. She is a co-winner of the 2018 Brunel International African Poetry Prize. She is the current Young People's Laureate for London and a columnist-in-residence at the San Francisco Museum of Modern Art's *Open Space*.

Ottessa Moshfegh is the author of the novella *McGlue*, the novel *Eileen* (shortlisted for the 2016 Man Booker Prize), and the short-story collection *Homesick for Another World*. Her new novel, *My Year of Rest and Relaxation*, was published in 2018. She lives in California.

Sayaka Murata's work has been awarded the 2009 Noma Prize for New Writers, the 2013 Yukio Mishima Prize and the 2016 Akutagawa Prize. Her novel, *Convenience Store Woman*, is now available in English, published by Portobello Books in the UK and Grove Atlantic in the US.

TaraShea Nesbit's first novel, *The Wives of Los Alamos*, was a finalist for the 2015 PEN/Robert W. Bingham Prize and a *New York Times* Editors' Choice. Her second novel, *Beheld*, will be published in 2020. She teaches at Miami University.

Brittany Newell's debut novel *Oola* was published in 2017. She is a regular contributor to *Dazed* magazine.

Tommi Parrish is a cartoonist, illustrator and art editor based in Montreal, whose second work and first longform graphic novel, *The Lie and How We Told It*, was published in 2018.

Sally Rooney is an Irish writer and the editor of *Stinging Fly*. She is the author of two novels, *Conversations with Friends* and *Normal People*, forthcoming from Faber & Faber.

Tomoko Sawada is a Japanese artist. She has been awarded the 2000 Canon New Cosmos of Photography Excellence Prize, the 2004 ICP Infinity Award and the 2004 Kimura Ihei Memorial Photography Award. Her work has been exhibited in Tokyo, London, Houston, New York and elsewhere.

Ginny Tapley Takemori's translations include works by Ryu Murakami, Miyuki Miyabe and Sayaka Murata.

Miriam Toews is a Canadian writer. Her novels include *A Complicated Kindness*, *Irma Voth* and *All My Puny Sorrows*, which was shortlisted for the 2015 Folio Prize and the 2015 Wellcome Book Prize. 'Women Talking' is taken from a novel of the same title which will be published by Faber & Faber in the UK, Bloomsbury in the US and Knopf in Canada.

Lisa Wells is the author of *The Fix*, winner of the 2017 Iowa Poetry Prize, and a book of essays, *Believers*, forthcoming from Farrar, Straus & Giroux. She lives in Seattle.

Zoe Whittall's third novel, *The Best Kind of People* was shortlisted for the 2016 Scotiabank Giller Prize. Her next novel, *The Spectacular*, is forthcoming in 2019.

Leni Zumas is the author of two novels, *Red Clocks* and *The Listeners*, and a story collection, *Farewell Navigator*. She lives in Portland, Oregon, and teaches in the MFA programme at Portland State University.